Pinpoint Inc.

Copyright © 2006 J. P. McCauley
All rights reserved.
ISBN: 1-4196-3663-4
Library of Congress Control Number : 2006903985

To order additional copies, please contact us.
BookSurge, LLC
www.booksurge.com
1-866-308-6235
orders@booksurge.com

Pinpoint Inc.

J. P. McCauley

2006

Pinpoint Inc.

CHAPTER ONE

HAROLD ANDREWS

The state of New York can be very cold in January. On this chilling day, dark gray clouds slowly rolled across the sky showing scattered hints of white highlights between the dark shadows. Muted threads of sunlight came shining through those dark moving shadows. It was a day to remind you that you are not living in the sunny south.

Inside Harold Andrews' luxury Lincoln Continental the temperature was a cozy 73 degrees, the correct temperature for self-important people. His car was a steel gray four-door sedan with lush gray leather seats. The seat covers were a little darker than Harold's graying hair. His six-foot frame, with a small potbelly, fit comfortably in the driver's heated seat. In fact, his lower body melted into the seat nicely. At 47 years old, he was in the prime of his career, had more money than most, and was certainly living the good life.

The car was headed north on New York interstate 87 towards the Buckhead Mountains and his private hunting lodge. His hunting retreat was certainly something much more than a cabin or cottage. It was a lodge big enough to sleep twelve to fifteen people in pure luxury. It was a hunting haven with all the comforts of home, something only the very wealthy could afford. The lodge was several miles west of the town of Catskill, a prime hunting area in upper New York State.

Although Harold had worked hard in achieving his position,

it didn't hurt that he had been born in an upscale area of New York City and had lived a life of a rich, spoiled child. There were few signs of love or affection in his family because his parents were too busy feeding their own personal egos. Mother was very active in women's clubs and organizations. She was a figurehead at the country club and heavily involved in women's rights of all kinds. Harold's father was a successful bank President in upper Manhattan. He was a man of few words and had lots of rules for those around him. Harold went only to private schools and took advantage of his family's status in the community. In high school he was involved in the debate club and the Deca club. He had no interest in sports, except that he did enjoy hunting. It was mandatory that he accompany his father to hunting clubs each fall.

Now a wealthy adult, Harold was actually a really rich boor without much personality. His interests while growing up were confined to individual activities that pleased him. He did not like group sports or group activities because they gave too much satisfaction to too many other people. He always wanted more than anyone else, and did not like being directed or controlled by anyone.

When he went to Harvard to study finance he socialized only with people who acknowledged his caste. He grew to love hunting because it was known as the sport of kings. He did not hunt squirrels and rabbits because they were easily available for the lower classes.

Harold had been quite successful in learning the basic principles of business. His focus was always on finance because it was a clear path to power and elite positions. He had watched his father and could see the personal returns that come with placing your own interest first.

Earlier in the day Harold had another very unpleasant

breakfast with his wife Helen. She was not his loving wife; she was just his wife. Helen was well aware of her standing in life and always found great pleasure in assuring that people understood her rank in local society. She was a tall, attractive, thin woman with rather sharp features. Her hair was natural blonde except for a few strands of gray on one side of her mid-length hairstyle. Her stately, rich look included small breasts and no pronounced rear end. She rather enjoyed living in her gated compound house, in a very affluent neighborhood. All in all, the air of wealth fit her style. Her only beauty flaws were crows' feet around her eyes and a slightly receding hairline.

With all her material wealth, she was constantly saddened that Harold paid little attention to their marriage. Making Helen feel comfortable and wealthy was an ongoing effort that Harold considered his greatest gift to her. However, this was not the gift she most wanted from him. What she wanted from Harold was a husband's love or at least an occasional sign of affection. She seldom received either from her husband.

The morning had begun with still another argument regarding his obvious lack of attention and affection.

"Harold, we have to talk. The amount of time you spend away from me and your home has increased to the point that I can no longer accept," she said in her usual tone of disdain. To Harold her voice was a sound like that of scraping nails against a blackboard. Her "performance" was typical and carried to a point at which Harold walked out of the room.

In a controlled anger she said: "I am damn tired of sitting in this big cold house waiting for you to include me in your life. I'm here alone with a maid and a television set and I'm tired of watching "Days of our Lives." During this little show she angrily continued to spin her five-caret wedding ring around and around on her slim, bony finger.

Even though she had acted out this little scene on numerous occasions, she still raged in a nervous, frigid manner. "I know you work hard and I have everything I need. Or maybe I should say, you work hard and you have everything you need, because I'm just another possession along with your precious business and hunting assets."

After a short pause and a stare-down, she continued with a closing verbal blow that probably should have been avoided. "You seem to have the delusion that I'm only here for whenever you find the time to 'act' like you are married, and your acting is pretty pitiful."

Harold interrupted with a loud shout that rumbled throughout the room, "That's enough!"

With the stare of a rabid dog ready to attack, he slowed his speech to a soft tone and added, "Do we have to do this every time we have breakfast together? Does breakfast time always mean it's time to tell me what an apparent ass I am? Can't you ever pull yourself together long enough to have a fresh thought and think of something else to say?"

He stood away from the table and continued in a slow, deliberate voice that backed her up a few steps. "So I spend a lot of time at work, big dam deal! I have to make one shit pot full of money just to keep you going! Have you looked at what your needs cost me lately? We have unbelievable florist bills, salon bills, jewelry bills, and country club bills

Hell, you could name any expensive item that pampers you and we will have a bill for it! Who could know what the hell you want? I never felt what I gave you was enough, you're all show."

With that, on cue, Harold stood up and stormed out of the room and straight to his bedroom where he packed his clothes and hunting gear for the trip to his private hunting lodge. She stood quietly spinning her wedding ring around her finger several times and glaring at the open doorway.

Thirty minutes later he was packed. There were no kisses goodbye as Harold walked out the doorway toward his car. He turned, looked back, and then got into his car. As he rolled down the window to say a forced goodbye, he noticed that Helen had walked to the opened car window and leaned forward with her fingernails digging the doorframe.

She looked like a woman scorned, a woman who was at her limit of disgust and anger. There seemed to be no love left in her thin, stately body. No love to give and none to take.

Harold spoke softly, "I'll be out working on the duck blinds for several days; I will call you when I get a chance." The only good thing about the moment was that he knew he would soon be driving away from her.

He added: "I want to give some thought to our pleasant conversation and try to figure out if there's any way possible to make you happy. I may not call you for a few days."

Before she could launch into another rage, he quickly raised his car window and drove his silver-gray Lincoln down the long driveway. With sweaty palms and his head shaking side to side, he was obviously in a hurry to get the hell away from her and her nasty hounding.

As he cruised up interstate 87, he thought little about Helen. He thought mostly of ducks and duck blinds. Reports earlier in the month from "Ducks Unlimited" stated that a record number of ducks would be traveling south to Mexico this season. His lodge in the Buckhead Mountains was not in the path of one of the main flyways. However, it was at least near a flyway that ducks sometimes used to fly from their breeding grounds in eastern Canada to their winter nesting area in Mexico.

As he drove, his thoughts drifted towards duck hunting,

making money and plans for what he wanted to do with the rest of his life. He had already convinced himself that keeping Helen happy shouldn't be his only lot in life. He was going to think about what makes Harold Andrews happy. As he reflected on Helen's place in his life, his last thoughts of her was: "That bitch probably wants to be divorced and a divorce would cost me a hell of a lot of my money."

As he drove through the suburbs towards the mountains, he also thought about his new "over and under" Remington shotgun and how he was hoping to make the duck's annual flight from Canada to Mexico a lot shorter than they expected. He also wondered if ducks give any thought at all about flying to Mexico or when they plan to arrive.

He smiled as he drove. He even hummed a few ole standards, like Frank Sinatra's "My Way."

CHAPTER TWO

THE DISCOVERY

Four days later a rusty, light blue, 1979 Chevy Luv pick-up truck turned the corner on Main Street in Jasper, New York. The dusty truck, with faded blue paint and several signs of dents, slowly headed towards the sheriff's office across from the county court house.

The winter air was cold and crisp. The mid-morning fog was giving way to strings of sunlight that came peeping through the darker clouds. The old truck was puffing white exhaust from its tailpipe as the driver slowly turned into a slanted parking space in front of the sheriff's office. In what seemed like slow motion, an older man in overalls and a black and red plaid jacket slid out of the front seat and down to the ground. His face was stern and rugged and carried a sense of real concern. With a deliberate motion he slammed the truck door closed, as if the latch might not work. He checked the closed door, and being satisfied that the latch actually worked, walked slowly to the entrance of the sheriff's office.

After peering though the cloudy door window and seeing no life inside, he checked the handle and found it unlocked. He walked in. The dim, tan light bulbs gave the room a rather dark and gloomy glow. It was a Sheriff office that reminded you of Mayberry USA.

The building, built out of old red brick, matched most of the other buildings in town. Jasper probably resembles many of towns in the area, prosperous in years past, but now in decline. It was a classic rural farming town with miles of flatland running up to the edge the mountains.

"Anyone home?" shouted the old man.

A startled "Huh, what!" blurted out, along with a clamor that sounded like pieces of paper and other office products falling off a table onto a wooden floor.

After a moment of silence the old man heard a response, "Sure, over here." The reply came from a corner desk further back in the dimly-lit room.

The old man was fairly certain he had awakened someone. He lowered his voice. "Is Sheriff Frey in?" he said. As he walked toward the desk, he could tell that the half-awake man behind it seemed to be caught in mid air between a decision either to stand up or stay seated.

After looking rather confused, the seated man made his decision and snapped to attention. "Nope, the Sheriff has gone to Albany on official business for a few days. I'm his new deputy, Frank Barns."

"Well, Frank Barns, I guess I'm just gonna have to talk to you, aren't I?"

"I guess you will," replied the unsure deputy in a rather official tone. "I'm in charge till the sheriff gets back. Whatever happens round here,
while the sheriff is gone, is my business. Now sit right over here and tell me what I can do for you."

The old man thought to himself, "God, there's nothing worse than a half—smart little man with a big sense of authority."

Realizing that he must deal with the situation as he found it, he proceeded with his comments.

"Well, Deputy Frank Barns, it's like this. While I was driving down the road towards my property over on route 27,

I noticed a bunch of tree limbs piled up fairly high just off my fence line. They were about twenty feet off the road. I notice those type things, you know, because these winters can tear the hell out of fences if you let debris pile up too close. Yes sir, I watch my fences real close."

"The branches were piled high and real thick. I know they weren't there a few days ago, so I checked them out. When I got to the stack of branches, I noticed that something shiny was underneath, kinda looked like a car."

"Was it a car?" the deputy asked excitedly.

"Yes, it was a car," replied the ole man in a curious voice while smiling at the excitement of the Deputy.

The old man continued, "Don't you want to know my name, Frank?"

"Sure, what's your name?" Frank blurted out as if he had already thought of asking a simple question like that. However, he didn't wait for the old man to answer.

"What kinda car was it? Is it still there?" With that, the deputy gathered a notepad, as if he was going to write down something very official.

"Yes, Frank, it's still there and my name is Gordon Dunbar. I own a farm and some acreage over on Highway 27."

"How long has it been there? Well, I mean, do you think it's been there a long time?" asked Deputy Frank.

Gordon knew the deputy was asking questions in the wrong order, but let it go.

"Well, Frank, it's been there long enough for the leaves to start turning brown on the dead branches...I'd say maybe three or four days."

"Did you look in the car? Was anyone in the car?" asked Frank.

"I didn't see anything in the car, but I couldn't see in very well. A lot of branches are covering the car and I didn't want to disturb anything or mess up any clues."

"Course not," the deputy replied. "Can you tell me anything else about the car? Did you look in the trunk?"

"Good Lord, Frank, no, I did not look in the trunk. I just told you I didn't want to disturb any evidence!"

"Do you think there might be fowl Play?" the deputy said softly.

"Yes, Frank, I think there might be some fowl play. I could see through the wilting leaves that the car has a bunch of bullet holes in the driver's side door. Why don't you just drive out there and see for yourself? I'll show you where it is."

Trying now to sound official, Deputy Frank Barns sternly asked, "Think I need to get some more deputies?"

"I don't think so, Frank, you just might be able to handle this all by yourself for now. But you might want to take your notepad just in case you want to write something down that might be important. And, you might want to make some arrangements to have the car towed into town after you check things out."

"Good idea, Mr. Dunbar, let me get my coat and gun. I'll just call over to the court house and let them know that I'll be gone on official business for a while."

"You do that, Frank," Gordon said with a slight grin.

A few minutes later Gordon Dunbar and Deputy Frank Barns were on their way to the area where the mystery car was hidden. Gordon was in his pick up truck and Frank in his "official" sheriff car with a siren and big red lights on the roof.

Although Frank had offered Gordon the opportunity to ride in the sheriff car, Gordon wasn't impressed nor did he want to drive all the way back to Jasper just to retrieve his truck. Gordon made the decision on separate cars and was insistent. Frank Barnes never challenged the idea.

It took about twenty minutes to reach the sight when Gordon slowed his truck and motioned back to the deputy to pull off the road and park. Both men got out of their vehicles and walked towards the fence. The cold air caused visible puffs of breath as they hurried toward the hidden car.

"It's right over there," Gordon said, pointing towards a wooden fence stretching about fifty yards in both directions.

The Deputy noticed the pile of branches as soon as Gordon pointed in that direction. "Yea, I see the pile of bushes. You sure they have only been there a few days?"

"You're the detective," Gordon said. "What does it look like to you?"

"I think they've been here for four or five days," he said. "They're start'en to turn brown, that's how you can tell," he continued, as if he had just figured it out all by himself.

"I guess you're right, Frank," Gordon grunted as they walked straight to a small opening in the pile of branches.

"Look right in here," Gordon said, pulling back a couple branches. "See right there on the lower part of the driver's door? It looks like several bullet holes to me. Looks like they sprayed the whole side of the car trying to shoot whoever was driving. They weren't good shots. Sure shot a little low."

The deputy now had most of his upper body leaning through the branches and his nose pressed almost against the driver's window.

"Ain't anybody in here, ain't nobody in the front or the back seat. None of the windows are broken either. Hey, whoever put this car here even locked the doors," Gordon observed, keeping his distance and not knowing just how involved he wanted to get in this whole thing.

"You gonna look in the trunk?" Gordon asked.

"Wish I had a key," the deputy replied. "I hate like hell to have to pry that damn trunk open. Maybe before I do anything I better take some pictures of the whole scene."

Furrowed brows appeared on the deputy's face, indicating that he was in deep thought. "The first thing the sheriff is going to ask me is if I stopped to think about things before jumping in and making a mistake. Did that once before on my last job and that's kinda why I'm in Jasper; ain't going to do it again."

Deputy Barns retrieved an old Cannon Sure Shot from his official sheriff car and proceeded to snap several pictures from various angles. After several brief walks around the hidden car and a few prodding pokes into the bushes, the Deputy asked Gordon to help remove the branches.

"Let's start with the branches on the back of the car," the deputy said. "I want to find out if anything's in the trunk. If someone's in there, I may need to call the corner's office in Jasper. God, I hope it's empty!"

With those comforting comments Frank and Gordon started throwing off branches from the rear of the car. When the back half of the car was clear, Frank and Gordon both said the same thing at the same time, "Lincoln Continental!"

After a couple seconds of hesitation, the deputy started prying the trunk with a tire tool, but with no luck. He couldn't budge the trunk lid, but did make one hell of a mess out of the trunk seam and the paint job.

He went back to his sheriff car and called the county courthouse on his car radio. The courthouse was the official back up contact when nobody was in the sheriff office. The deputy told the gal on duty where he was on official business and asked her to contact the local garage for assistance. She, in turn, relayed the deputy's message to Sid Clayton, who owned the local garage and was the best mechanic in Jasper. In fact, he was the owner of the only tow truck in the county.

PINPOINT INC.

Frank and Gordon were sitting in Frank's car finishing a cup of semi-cold coffee when Sid's tow truck finally arrived.

Sid parked the truck along the fence line and walked towards the two men in the parked car. "Whatcha got Frank?" he asked, giving a second look at Gordon sitting in the passenger's seat. "I understand you've got a car someone found hidden, do you know whose car it is?"

"Nope," Frank replied. "We don't know whose car it is. I asked Sue in the Courthouse to call the Sheriff's office in Albany and give them the license plate number. I gave it to her when I had her call you. We should find out soon, Sue's going to call me on the car radio. What we need to do now is get the trunk open on the car. You have anything in your tow truck for that job?"

"Should be no problem," Sid answered.

Within ten minutes Sid had the trunk lock open, but the lid was still down. The deputy moved fairly slowly to the trunk lid and as he lifted it very slowly, all three men leaned over and followed the trunk lid up. As they all peered in the trunk they could see it contained a spare tire, a small toolbox, a set of jumper cables and an Indianapolis, Indiana phone directory.

It did not contain dead bodies, bloodstains or any hints of fowl play. With some feeling of relief, the three men cleared the tree limbs and debris. After the car was clear it was hooked up to the tow truck. Sid took the mystery car back to his garage for safekeeping until a real investigation on the car could be conducted.

Deputy Frank Barnes and Gordon Dunbar exchanged pleasant remarks, shook hands, and went their separate ways.

The next morning TV Channel 11, Eyewitness News in New York City, broke their lead story with a sense of international intrigue: "Authorities in upstate Jasper, New York, discovered an empty, bullet-ridden Lincoln sedan yesterday just off state road #27, towards the town of Catskill. The luxury car was found hidden in bushes with several bullet holes in the driver side door. The car is registered to Andrews International Corporation of this city.

"Andrews International is a leading international investment-banking firm founded by current Board Chairman, 47-year-old Harold Andrews. Authorities, working with New York state police, are investigating the possible disappearance of Mr. Andrews, assuming he was the driver."

"Mrs. Andrews has acknowledged that her husband left several days ago for a hunting trip in the Buckhead mountains. She said that she has not heard from him since, but stated that she was not alarmed by the fact that he hadn't contacted her."

"Eyewitness news reporter, Dan Fair, reported that no blood stains were found in the car and that they had no information on who was driving the car. There also was no evidence of the whereabouts of Mr. Andrews. We will keep you updated as events unfold."

"This, is eyewitness news"

CHAPTER THREE

JASON HIGGINS

Seventeen years ago Jason Higgins was an 18-year-old high school senior in Carmel, Indiana, a bedroom community just north of Indianapolis. It is a community of successful business people who live in successful looking houses and raise successful, athletic children. The combination brings great attention to the local high school sports program.

Growing up in Indiana means that for the rest of your life you continue to explain what it means to be a "Hoosier." It's one of those little pieces of trivia that no one has ever been able to answer, even the people from Indiana. They put it on their auto license plates, on the signs of their retail stores and even use it to name their college athletic teams. Even with all that, nobody in Indiana knows exactly what it means. Whatever it means, it always brings a sense of pride to people from Indiana.

Being six-foot four, 200 pounds, blonde, very smart and good looking makes you a "Hunk' in any high school in America. However, also being an all-state high school basketball player in the state of Indiana means you got the world by the tail.

Jason was all that and more. As top student at Carmel High School, he was the one other students expected to be very successful in life. Being a top athlete was just a bonus. Jason could have been six foot, seven inches, if he had not turned under and worn a size 13 shoe.

Since Carmel High School was one of the top athletic and

academic schools in the state, most people interested in sports had a good chance to hear news or see Jason on television or read about him in the newspapers.

As a senior, he was the starting forward on the basketball team. The team went to the Indiana State High School basketball tournament and had won the sectional and regional championships. The next step was the semi-finals, which included eight teams from four parts of the state. After that, there would be four teams left in the tournament. They would be known as "The Final Four."

In Indiana, at that time, every high school was automatically in the state tourney regardless of school size. The teams would play in small geographic areas on the first weekend and the winners would go forward to play in a larger geographic area. On the third weekend the winners of the four semi-final locations would converge on Indianapolis to play as the "Final Four." Although just being in the overall tourney was a thrill, the ultimate dream of every young ball player in Indiana was to make it to Hinkel Fieldhouse in Indianapolis, and the Final four.

Jason was like every other boy in the state, he fantasized about shooting that last shot to win the Boys' High School Championship. It was born into the very fiber of most boys in Indiana. The old joke was that when a newborn boy leaves the hospital his first basketball is "issued" to him. Most Hoosiers jokingly thought it was a state law.

The tourney's final four was played in Indianapolis. Carmel lost to Jeffersonville in the first game by three points although Jason scored twenty-three points and had an outstanding game. It was, however, not enough to carry the team on to the championship game. Jason was disappointed, but looked forward to college basketball.

After that game his long-time girlfriend, Cindy Hassel, the best looking cheerleader in school history, suggested they visit a school parking lot behind Butler University in midtown Indianapolis. With the kiss of an angel and the lust of a teenage girl, before the night was over, she made loosing the game an unimportant issue. Cindy was five feet four, 118 pounds, with skin that always looked tan from sunbathing. Her hair was a beautiful silky blonde, sometimes pulled up on her head revealing what just might be the best looking "back of the neck" in the school. To top it all off, they were King and Queen at the senior prom.

Jason came form a very stable family. His father, Bert Higgins, was a senior executive with the Ely Lilly Corporation, one of the country's leading pharmaceutical firms, and located in Indianapolis. His family vacations included Rocky Mountain ski outings, European sight seeing trips, fishing excursions with his dad in Alaska and other exciting adventures most people only dream about.

Besides girls and sports, Jason's other loves were computers and law enforcement. In elementary school he always talked about being a policeman. In high school he broadened his goals to include all types of law enforcement, including using technology to control crime and criminals.

His plans for after high school were to earn a basketball scholarship to Indiana University and to play for Bobby Knight and the Hurrin' Hoosiers. He also wanted a degree in Criminology.

Towards the end of his senior year he came to his mom for advice.

"Mom, I haven't talked about this with dad, but I haven't had any contact from Indiana University about playing basketball."

"I know they've seen me play. I understand that they are

looking at a very strong recruiting class this year and it looks like I'm not in their plans. Maybe I should look at other schools. The only problem is, I want to go to Indiana. I've wanted to go for as long as I can remember."

After some casual conversation with his mom, it was decided to discuss it later with his dad. After discussions with his dad, an Indiana University graduate himself, Jason focused on Indiana University, regardless of his basketball opportunities.

As his high school senior year ended, Jason did not get his scholarship to play basketball at Indiana. He did, however, get academic scholarships to many schools, including Indiana University. The decision was made to attend Indiana and try to play basketball as a "walk on."

Jason enrolled in Indiana University in Bloomington that fall. Although he was a "walk-on" on the basketball team and got his chance to play for Bobby Knight, he did not make the final cut and did not make the team. He was heartbroken, but focused on his studies.

The Indiana coach's comments on Jason were that he was big, strong, smart, coordinated, a good shooter, but his feet were too slow on defense. His game was good for high school, but not good enough for Bobby Knight's "Hurrin' Hoosiers."

He sometimes missed his high school sweetheart Cindy, but time had passed them by. He had gone to Bloomington to school and she had stayed in Indianapolis to attend Butler University. When he left, they both thought they were in love, but the distance between the schools was just too great.

Even though they saw each other when Jason was home during school breaks, it just wasn't enough to keep the fires in their hearts burning. During the second semester they mutually agreed to date other people. Soon there was no romantic relationship at all.

Although he hadn't made the IU basketball team, at least he was attending the school he wanted and was soon a member of Delta Tau Delta Fraternity. With a 3.8 grade point average, Jason was smart and was doing very well on the university social scene. After his freshman year and during the rest of his summers he worked as a computer technology intern in Indianapolis.

In his senior year Jason became very intrigued with the connection between computer science and crime prevention. He believed that the future would involve preventing and fighting crime with the use of wireless technology, including intelligent computer chips and programs. The more Jason studied, the more he became hooked on the possibilities of making his life goal in the high tech computer field.

Surprising to nobody, Jason graduated on time and, without shifting any gears, went straight into graduate school, continuing to pursue his dream of fighting crime with technology.

At the end of his graduate program Jason wrote a wonderful thesis that evolved from his passion to control criminal activities through technology. His professors were highly impressed with his theory. His thesis was a stretch for most minds, but for Jason's, as clear as a bell. The entire idea started when he read an ad for the current "LoJack" auto-theft concept, an idea that had been successful.

Their premise was to place a small electronic device in an undetectable location of a car. The police, then, by activating the device, could trace the location of a car and recover it.

Jason took this concept a few steps further. Why not implant a "human—friendly" microchip in the world's most important people and protect them from emergencies such as accidents, terrorism and kidnapping. Many important people in the world today live lives that are intertwined with high risk and high responsibility. Jason's theory would include a highly developed microchip, activated and maintained by human body heat and capable of being traced anywhere in the world using a satellite tracking station. The microchip could be so small it could be hidden inside the body without a trace to the human eye. Upon Graduation, with graduate degrees in Computer Science and Criminology, Jason started looking for avenues to pursue his vision of a computerized chip and a global tracking system.

It doesn't hurt to have a father who is a senior officer in one of the world's largest companies. Within a few months Jason, with the help of his father, had developed an overview of what a company like this would need in the areas of capital and employees.

Since Jason was new to the business game, his Dad suggested he get a couple years of practical experience before he invested money in the business world. It was sound advice and Jason listened to his Dad.

CHAPTER FOUR

WINNING, LOOSING, WINNING

For the past five years, since college, Jason had been very busy consulting for the State of Indiana, Marion County and the city of Indianapolis. His main focus had been law enforcement enhancements. His main project had been the development and installation of Global Tracking Systems in state police posts, county police districts and local police stations. This included a new tracking system in each patrol car, including audio/visual systems that allowed the patrol cars to be monitored live at all times. In the past, patrol cars simply had video taping systems and recorded police procedures when stopping suspected lawbreakers. The new system would be live, and if any trouble occurred, backup help could respond immediately.

When he left Indiana University and settled in Indianapolis he leased a beautiful two-bedroom condo around the Keystone Crossing/Fashion Mall area in northern Indianapolis. The condo was about two blocks south of Keystone Avenue in a park-like setting. It was a two-story, traditional style with a basement leading out to a deck on a small lake. It was a well maintained complex of about twenty condos hidden away from the main roads and malls by large, beautiful trees and flowering bushes.

His décor and furnishings were geared towards the macho male. If you asked Jason what his favorite color was, he might say beige, because that was the only real color in his condo. The condo consisted of empty Chesty potato chip bags, empty Bud Lite beer cans and an Indiana University flag that hung on his bedroom wall.

The flag had a big white "I.U." in the center of a crimson background.Other than that, the condo was pretty dull. Too bad he didn't have a giant nude photo of Cindy Hassel. If he had that, the condo would not be dull.

Jason did have a personal passion for clothes. His closet was full of preppie items mainly purchased from a premium outlet mall thirty miles south of Indianapolis, close to Columbus, Indiana. The outlet mall had all the good stores——Ralph Lauren, Tommy Hilfiger, Brooks Brothers, Nautcia, Eddie Bauer and many others. Jason spent a lot of time and cash at the outlet, but it was one of his few shortcomings, so, what the hell.

During the early years in his condo, Jason had many young, beautiful ladies for dinner and drinks, sometime more. Most all visitors thought Jason might just be the catch of the century and were more than willing to show their affection in various ways. Although Jason was a fairly normal male, he always gave attention and interest to whomever he was with. However, he never passed up an opportunity to do research for the "Kinsey Report, "which happened to be located on the campus of Indiana University. As an I.U. student he always felt he wanted to contribute something to his school, and his personal research for Kinsey seemed appropriate and rather invigorating.

Then, fate intervened. Cindy, his old high school sweetheart, showed up again in his life. He had been in St. Elmo's restaurant in downtown Indianapolis eating a sixteen-ounce T-bone with a female friend when Cindy Hassel walked into the room with her date. They took a table just fifteen feet away from Jason's table.

If Jason looked slightly over the left shoulder of his date, and over the right shoulder of the man sitting behind his date, he would look directly into Cindy's beautiful face. His initial impression was that she might be even more beautiful than before.

It took a few minutes for Cindy to realize that someone was staring at her. She had not seen Jason when she came into the room. Looking straight ahead, Cindy noticed the man staring at her just a couple tables away. It had been several years since she had seen the boyfriend she had taken to the school bus in the parking lot after the big basketball game loss. There he was, the boy who had stolen her heart and then left for college while she stayed in Indianapolis.

Now here they were, once again realizing what they really meant to each other with just a mere series of glances. Later that week Jason would find Cindy's phone and address and their hearts would soon be one again.

His wonderful lifestyle and all that fun with Cindy lasted a little more than a year when a tragic event would happened. He would lose interest in shopping for clothes at the Columbus outlet or in eating breaded tenderloins sandwiches with friends at Broadripple's bars and grills. He would lose interest is getting together with friends at Guiest Reservoir for boating afternoons. In general, he would just lose interest in life. He would drink way too many vodka martinis.

Time passed and now six years after writing his thesis, Jason thought he might be ready and anxious to start his company. He went to his father's office at the Lilly Corporation on a rainy spring morning to discuss his next steps in life with his dad. Actually, he went to discuss the last year of his life with the man who had supported him most.

The last year was not a good year for Jason. The young man who had been on top of the world most of his life now had to gather himself together for a difficult discussion with his dad.

"Your father will see you now," said Martha, the attractive forty-yearold secretary in the executive office suites of the Eli Lilly Corporation.

"Thank you Martha," Jason said in a soft, low voice. "Is he in a good mood today?" He showed that smile that made younger women swoon, not to say that Martha didn't feel a little twinge for Jason now and then.

"He's always in a good mood when you come to see him. You doing OK, Jason? Your father has sure been worried about you".

He brought a twinkle to his eye along with another large smile to his face. "I'm fine, thanks. You're still the best looking gal in the company."

That brought a rather large blush to Martha's face, but she loved it.

Anyone seeing Bert Higgins' office had no doubt of his success at Eli Lilly. Not only was the office large with huge tinted windows, but the pile carpet, leather couch, oversized desk, along with the framed art and antiques, smartly stated his position. Bert was still as handsome as his son. His light brown hair was grayed at the temples and his face had attractive character lines. His striking eyes were bright baby blue and his six-foot two body was still sleek and trim. In addition to all these physical assets, probably most impressive were his mind and manners, which were still as sharp and graceful as ever.

"Hi Dad, how's Mom!" Jason blurted with the bright smile that his dad remembered from years past. Jason walked into his dad's office with arm and hand extended. They shook hands, but after a small awkward pause they hugged, as they always did. There was even a small kiss on each other's cheek.

Bert answered, "Mom's great, how are you doing?"

"I'm doing fine. I think getting back a normal life is all I need."

Bert answered with a large smirk on his face, "What the hell is a normal life these days? I'm not sure any of us can be normal with the economy and all the shit that's going on in the world."

He continued, "Son, I know it's been difficult, but you have to get over what happened. It was an accident and that's that! You've got too much to offer this world. It's really time to move on and start that adventure you have always dreamed of. Your idea is still great stuff."

"I know Dad. I know it's time. I've slowed my drinking down to a normal pace and the nightmares no longer keep me awake. I think with the help from a lot of people, I've come back to accepting what happened. The guilt will just have to go way when it goes away."

After a few more lighthearted comments about the upcoming Indianapolis Colts football season, they settled into some serious business talk.

"Son, I think you are in a position and have the opportunity to find that start-up capital you need for your new company. I have some sizable investments that I'm willing to use as collateral, assuming that if someday I am old and broke, you will take us in so we don't have to live on the street! Your Mom just wouldn't look very good pushing a shopping cart full of aluminum cans." Bert said with a slight chuckle.

They both laughed and Jason's old smile seemed to reappear. He sat back in the soft leather office chair and thought about what his father had just said. He remembered what things were like just a few months ago.

Bert looked at his son and remembered the little boy with the dirty sweat socks and the grimy tennis shoes. The little boy who loved to sit at the kitchen table and shoot rolled up paper wads into the waste paper basket on the other side of the kitchen. He was the little boy who wanted to be a basketball star and play at Indiana for Bobby Knight.

"After they came out of their thoughts, Bert said, " Ok Son, let's do it!"

"OK dad, Let's do it!"

After some detailed discussion on the construction of a proposed corporate structure, office space, employee requirements, a corporate mission statement and a few other details necessary to write a proposal for potential investors, the meeting was over.

On the drive back to his condo, Jason reflected on his family and all the painful events of the last several months.

He recalled his proposal to Cindy, a very romantic proposal that finallycame after all those years of on and off again dating. He remembered her acceptance and the announcement that brought tears to all their old college friends at the St. Valentine's party. He remembered all the long discussions about her teaching English at Broad Ripple High School and his building his company and his dream.

Then he recalled the spring weekend night on his 22 foot Bayliner boat, on Giest reservoir, just northeast of Indianapolis. He thought of all the laughing, all the fun and the unfortunate heavy drinking that day and evening. He remembered the sun going down and wanting the day to just go on and on. He remembered letting nightfall come and consume their discussions and of not having a care in the world and forgetting to turn on the boat's running lights.

Then, with their boat drifting out in the cool, dark spring night, he recalled what sounded like a trolling motor, maybe on a boat far away. Then the sound suddenly changed to a large engine roar. Natural instinct made him jump to the back of the boat with the thought of turning on the running lights. He also had the helpless thought that he had left Cindy sitting in the middle of the boat.

Next was the terrible sound of disintegrating fiberglass when the speeding boat slashed through the east side of Jason's boat, splitting it in half and throwing him backwards into the blackened waters of Giest Reservoir.

Next was confusion and disorientation followed by thoughts of helplessness. Next was the panic of not knowing what happened. The next thing was to find Cindy, but not knowing which way to go. Lastly, wasthe realization that all there was to do was to try and stay afloat.

People in other boats came to help. His first fear came when he realized he was alone in the water, but the heart wrenching pain came when he realized that Cindy was nowhere to be seen in the water.

It was not until the next day when rescue officers found what was at one time Cindy Hassel. When the entire event settled in his mind, he found he had no interest in life. His life had been altered forever.

The funeral was hard to really remember. It was an event that seemed untrue or unreal. It seemed like he was somewhere far removed during the funeral, but thought that when he did return, all would be well.

After the funeral, as he turned into his condo driveway,

he snapped back to reality and reverted back into a deep depression.

What he now remembers, all too well, was the depression, self-pity, anger and a whole lot of alcohol. Sadly, the alcohol did not bring Cindy back or make life more bearable. The alcohol did, however, remove any social life he might have had. As far as he could see, nothing important was going to happen with his life from that point on.

When he hit bottom, as people always do, he slowed his drinking, cleared his thinking, and like a lifting fog, there he was, still alive. He knew he had to do something constructive. Life was still a bitch, but the sun was starting to shine through.

CHAPTER FIVE

THE COMPANY

Seven years after writing his thesis Jason had his dream of building his company well on track. It was time for another visit to his father's office. He greeted his father's secretary.

"Hi Martha, how's the best looking woman at Eli Lilly doing? he said.

"Oh Jason, you smooth talker, you, if I was a few years younger and not your father's secretary I'd give those young girlfriends of yours a run for their money."

"But Martha, the problem is there aren't any young girlfriends in my life. You would have smooth sailing."

"That just means there's a lot of dumb, blind, women in Indianapolis," She quipped.

Hearing all the conversation, but not the words, Bert Higgins appeared inthe doorway.

"What's all the chatter out here? Martha, if you're making a pass at my son, I'm telling you right now, I'm not going to be your father-inlaw!"

Martha's face turned a deep red and Jason broke into a laugh.

"Get in here, son, before you do something you'd regret the rest of your life!"

That brought another giggle from Martha and another big smile from Jason.

After some more small talk about the ho-hum season the

Indianapolis Colts had this year, Jason told his father about the financial commitments they had received for his new company.

"I have five commitments for one million dollars each. Each one from a different financial investor, but they all are very much alike. We have one each from New York, New Jersey, Connecticut, Rhode Island and Massachusetts. It is really interesting that they all have the same investment requirements and guidelines. The papers we completed for each had the same questions and required information. They were all done through an investment broker. At least it made it easier to complete; you just gathered the information for one and used it over and over again."

Jason smiled and said, "You and I can sign the papers in the next few weeks and we'll be on our way to making Pinpoint Inc. come alive."

"Pinpoint, Inc.?" Dad replied. "Where did that come from, I thought you had decided on Higgins Inc. Ya know, the family name and all that."

"Well dad, I know you wanted to use our name, but I thought using a name that reflected what we did as a company, it might be a better marketing tool."

With an approving head nod from dad, Jason continued, "I have found a chief financial officer and a great marketing officer. I will make them offers next week."

"When I talked to John Lewis, my future marketing guru, he suggested the name change from Higgins, Inc. to Pinpoint, Inc. and I agreed. All the paperwork we file for the investment capital will be with the name Pinpoint, Inc."

"I think it's a great idea, Jason, it makes a lot of sense," Dad replied.

Jason continued, "What I need to do now is hire my human resources director and start putting the rest of the team together.

I've found space just north of town, around Meridian and 110th street. It should be all the space we need for now and has room on both sides of the building to expand."

Jason softened his excitement and said, "The real challenge is finding a research director and a medical director. The medical position may not be difficult, but the research director will have to bring some individual talent in the computer science and biotech fields. That may be a real challenge for us to find. We are somewhat lucky that much of the technology has already been discovered; all we have to do is direct that technology towards our needs. I have contacted a head hunter and hopefully he can find someone soon."

"What technology is already available?" Dad asked.

"Well, the computer chip that we'll need for human implantation is very similar to the ones now being used on pets like cats and dogs, but we'll have to make sure the human body will not reject the chip. I think we can take what is available today and within a few months redesign it to meet our needs."

"What's the chance of human body rejection?"

Jason paused. "Well, I have no earthly idea at this point, but I do know it can be done. We'll just have to find the best research doctors available, have them work with our computer tech people and hope they can design what we need. We will probably need more than one person. That's why the initial overhead investment is going to go through the roof. It's going to take some time, but we'll do it. I also have the head hunter looking for other positions we will need filled." Jason sounded more confident and excited than ever.

Two weeks later Jason flew to San Francisco, rented a car and drove south on Bayshore Dr., then to the famous highway 101 and Palo Alto, the home of Stanford University.

Jason had rented a room at the Crowne Plaza for his interview. It was the best hotel in the area.

The room had a sitting area separate from the bedroom. The sitting area had a table and four chairs along with a couch and a lounge chair. It had a larger television than a normal hotel room. The room was located on the Concierge floor, which meant that down the hall was a lounge room with complimentary food and drinks and a large screen television. It was a perfect lounge for interviewing, especially young women who might be a little uneasy sitting in a hotel room with a man they didn't really know.

The phone rang; it was a call from the hotel lobby. Jason gave the caller the floor and room number of the concierge room. Five minutes later a knockout young lady walked into the room. Jason rose to greet her.

"Hello, Paula, my name is Jason Higgins." "Hello, Mr. Higgins, I'm Paula Higginbothem, but people call me Higgie. I've never been real fond of the name Paula."

To break the ice, Jason said, "That's a very interesting last name, Paula, or should I say, Higgie; we both have names that start with the same six letters. Mine is Scotch-Irish; what's yours?"

"I'm not real sure, Mr. Higgings. I know my family came from both England and Ireland, but I'm not very sure exactly where."

"Well, Higgie, my family came from Ireland back in the late 1800's. In fact, the name was originally O'Higgins. I suspect somebody probably got drunk on their way to America and upon arrival, spelled it wrong. Maybe the custom people wrote it wrong. Anyway, it's now just Higgins."

After interviewing Higgie regarding her educational background and questions limited to what the government will allow you to ask about her personal life, Jason felt like he had a winner.

He had already done his homework on her entire background. She was from Monterey, California, and her parents were both educators. She was thirty years old, five foot four, with long blonde hair and a face that belonged in Playboy and the body to go with it. She graduated high school and Stanford with honors, which means she's got a brain full of information and facts. She was not your typical blue-eyed, blonde California surfer girl who only looks for fun and instant gratification. She played tennis and golf and actually understood the basic principles of basketball and football. She even liked to backpack and climb mountains. The real clincher for Jason was that she liked to fish. A girl who can pick up a juicy worm and put it on a hook is a girl who can do almost anything.

As he looked at her he thought to himself, "Dear God, what more could you want in a woman? Maybe I should be dating her rather than hiring her."

However, what he needed more than a date at this point in his life was a Technical Director with a brain.

Jason said, "Higgie, I'm putting together a company in Indianapolis Indiana, named Pinpoint Inc. Maybe you already know that from the head hunter. I'm looking for someone to lead the effort to develop a microchip that can be implanted in the human body and be detected worldwide using computer satellite systems. That's about as plain as I can make it at this time."

He continued, "I know you have a Masters and Ph.D. in Computer Science from Stanford, which puts you in the upper echelon of people in this field. I also assume you are well qualified for what I am looking for. What I don't know is, if you want to take on a big challenge like this and live in Indiana."

"Well, Mr. Higgins, I did a little research on you also. The head hunter you hired told me enough about you and your plans and allowed me to give this position some serious thought before this interview."

Jason was impressed. "The head hunter I hired does not know much about the details of what the company will do, just the basic requirements of the type of person we are looking for."

"Well, Mr. Higgins, give me some credit. You are looking for some-one with an educational background that is very technical and you do not have a company or a product at this time. It doesn't take a rocket scientist to figure out that whoever takes this job will have to help develop the product and be an important part of the company. That sounds like a real challenge to me."

"What about living in Indiana?" Jason asked with a hopeful tone of voice.

"Other than the fact that Indiana doesn't have large mountains to climb, they do play basketball there, don't they?" she replied with a big smile.

"They've been known to toss a few balls towards a basket hanging on a barn wall," Jason replied.

As far as Jason was concerned the interview was over. It was just a matter of salary and benefits. If she agreed to the offer, he had himself one hell of a Research Director. They both departed in good sprits, with an agreement to keep in touch.

Two days later Jason called Higgie to make an offer. She accepted. Three weeks later she was in Indianapolis.

It wasn't long before the head hunter found Jason two medical directors. Things were rolling right along for Pinpoint, Inc.

PINPOINT INC.

The first doctor was Lloyd Roper. He was a graduate of Brown University with an M.D./Ph.D. in Medical Biology and Genetics. Dr. Roper was pudgy, white headed, middle-aged, with a fun and jovial personality. He had been in the research department at Brown University for several years. He and his wife were empty nesters and he was getting bored with his work. He was looking for a new challenge and maybe more money for retirement. His background and personality fit Jason's plans quite nicely. The offer was made and accepted. Jason had landed another important team member.

The second important medical find was Dr. Trammell Waller. Waller was a graduate of the University of Tennessee's medical school in Memphis. Dr Waller had graduated a long time ago and had many problems in his life. However, one problem he didn't have was a lack of medical knowledge and skills. He was very proficient at internal medical procedures and surgery. He and his wife had marriage problems because of his alcohol consumption and inability to cope when under pressure. All in all, he did not sound like a good prospect. However, he was widely known to be very competent when he was not having personal problems. The fact that he was now working in Indianapolis at St Vincent's hospital would mean there would be no relocating cost and, if things didn't work out, Jason could always let him go. Besides he had Dr. Roper on board to keep an eye on him.

Only one more part of the staff puzzle was left to complete. Jason needed a wiz at computers and satellite systems.

Two weeks later the head hunter contacted Jason with information on an outstanding candidate for this computer/satellite wiz.

The good news was that the man possessed all the skills and knowledge Jason wanted. The bad news was that he had graduated from Purdue in Lafayette Indiana. Jason joked with the head hunter that since the guy had degrees from Purdue, he could be paid less salary since his education couldn't be that good! It was a long-standing joke between Indiana and Purdue graduates. Bloomington and Lafayette were only ninety miles apart.

Both schools were in the Big Ten conference and the rivalry was so intense they might as well have been in the same town. In reality, students and alumni slamming each other was really a fun part of the rivalry, unless, of course, it was football or basketball season and you're playing each other. During those times things could get a little more serious.

One week later Jason was on his way to Lafayette to interview Jim Kraft.

He knew that Kraft had what he needed and if he had to, he would salute the Purdue colors of black and gold to get him. It might hurt down deep, but sometimes you just have to do what you have to do. He would not mention that Bobby Knight and the Hurrin' Hoosiers had kicked the crap out of Purdue's basketball team just a week ago.

He liked Jim Kraft. Jokes were exchanged when the interview started. That was good because if they were to work together, they both would have to take a little "ribbin" now and then. Jim was around forty, a sports fan, married with two children, and possessed a brilliant mind.

Three days later Jim Kraft accepted the offer and was the newest member of the Pinpoint, Inc. team. With most of the team was in place, it was time to research and produce.

Jason had used another "head hunter' to find a Marketing Director. John Lewis had great credentials, with a marketing degree from Michigan State. After two interviews, John was on board.

His last major need was someone to handle the money. His dad recommended a man who had interviewed at Eli Lilly. As soon as Jason told his dad what he needed, dad had the answer. Sid Worthington.

Sid held a Masters Degree from Penn State. After college he had come to Indianapolis to work for Bank of America. He had liked his job, but banking wasn't quite as exciting as working with products or building a company, so he interviewed with Eli Lilly, who was starting a new division. Even though he came in second for the job, Bert Higgins was highly impressed with Sid. Bert thought Sid was a financial wiz and if dad thought that, it was good enough for Jason.

CHAPTER SIX

THE MICROCHIP AND TRACKING PROGRAM

Jason Higgins held his first staff meeting at Pinpoint, Inc. Attending was Research Director Higgie Higginbothem, Research Medical Director Dr. Lloyd Roper, Medical Services Director Dr. Trammell Waller, Technical Director Jim Kraft, Marketing Director John Lewis, and Chief Financial Officer Sid Worthington.

Jason usually wore casual clothes at work unless he was meeting someone from outside the company. Today he had on gray slacks, a light blue, button-down, polo dress shirt, a Brooks Brothers navy blazer and Cole Hann black loafers. A real Dapper Dan. He was dressed this way because he was the boss and younger than many attending the meeting. It was his edge of authority because everyone else was dressed casually.

Jason had already written and re-written the product development plan and, with the help of Marketing Director John Lewis, had written a marketing plan.

"Good morning and welcome to Pinpoint Inc." Chairman Jason Higgins said to his new team. "Coffee and donuts are on the table, and I plan to have these meetings on a regular basis. I have given each of you a written product development plan and a marketing plan. As you can see, we have our work cut out for us."

A few moans and groans came from the group, but all with smiles and grins. It was a happy, fun group.

Jason continued, "None of us are getting any younger and we need to start producing some income in the near future. The bottom line is that we need to proceed with some urgency." Jason tried to keep his voice firm, but friendly.

"Our first task is for Higgie and her team to research all current development and conventional technology that would involve computerized micro-chips. We are looking to develop our own human-friendly microchip that has the additional capability of monitoring body temperature."

"Jim Kraft and his tech team will have to research and develop a computer satellite system that can track our microchip anywhere in the world. Hopefully, down to a square, city block."

"Our two doctors, Lloyd and Trammell, will research and work with Higgie to make sure the microchip is compatible with the human body and the various locations in the human body the microchip can be placed in a human body for maximum security."

"Lastly, but of great importance, Jim Lewis will continue to develop a marketing plan that identifies a potential client list. As you know, the overall marketing plan is to offer our product and services to highly visible and invaluable people working in government, corporations, business and industry. This could include industry leaders, heads of state, governors, senators, congressmen, celebrities, presidents, chairmen or any other person who could be at risk to be lost or kidnapped."

"Ok, are there any questions or comments?" Jason asked.

Higgie asked, "Who is going to do the pricing and develop the fee structure?"

Jason replied, "Sid and I are working on that now, but we

will have to get a better feel for our research and development costs before we can estimate any fees."

Sid added, "It's our feeling that large corporations, governments and industries wanting to protect their investments and their key people won't have too much trouble paying a substantial start up fee and ongoing monthly service fees."

The Technical Director, Jim Kraft, spoke up, "How long can we last with our current financial assets before we need to start producing revenue?"

"Jason replied, "Well, that depends on how efficient you are with your allocated budgets. If you drag your feet and your personal expense statements go through the roof with outrageous meals and travel, then we may be in some trouble."

Then, with a big smile, he added, "Unless, of course, I'm with you!"

The group chuckled.

"Anything else?" Jason said. "Let's get together next Monday morning at nine o'clock to see where we are. The many opportunities for this company are ours to discover." With that last bit of inspiration, he adjourned the meeting. The staff cheerfully went their separate ways.

To Jason's delight the entire team worked at a furious pace, sometimes late into the evening and sometimes on Saturdays. Weeks went by and the company game plan seemed to be on track. Jason was happy with the work and progress in all areas.

After six months of testing, Higgie announced that she was ready to test the effect of the microchip in the body of a human. The question was, which human? After considering soliciting medical research volunteers from the general public, Jason decided the financial risk, via lawsuits, was too great and volunteered himself.

After detailed meetings with Higgie and Dr. Waller, who

would perform the implant, Jason had the first microchip implanted in his upper body area, under his right armpit. The minor surgery was quick and easy. The medical research team didn't seem to think that the location on the body would make much difference for body reception and, at this point, was fairly certain that the body wouldn't reject the microchip.

Jason's microchip was much smaller than a shirt button and implanted just below the skin surface. The incision would be so small that in a matter of days the entry scar would completely disappear. As a security precaution, future implants would be in various locations on the bodies of clients. This would assure that no captors or terrorists could discover the microchip by visual sight. Detailed charts would be kept on each client showing the exact location of their microchip. All records and charts would be kept secure in a vault at Pinpoint, Inc.

After two days Jason developed a slight redness where the chip was located. After an injection of a common antibiotic, the redness disappeared.

It was noted in their research files that a small dose of antibiotic should be given when microchips are implanted. Within a few days there was no visible incision scar.

At the next staff meeting Jason asked Marketing Director John Lewis to brief the group on the initial plans to market the microchip.

John came to the head of the table where the computerized overhead projector was located. "We are really excited about our opportunities to market Pinpoint, Inc. To date, we have developed a lot of early interest by talking to selective, potential clients. It seems that not only do clients who want to protect themselves have a personal interest, but also corporate boards and other leaders whose business or government would suffer greatly with the disappearance or death of a key colleague."

John continued, "With this information we are able to develop a potential client list that will keep us busy for a long time. Once we establish ourselves as a creditable organization, with a reliable product, we expect 'word of mouth' to help sell our product and service."

John then concluded by using the overhead projector to list some of the potential clients that had given feedback. They included founders of companies and corporations, heads of state of foreign countries, key governmental leaders on the federal and state levels, people in the entertainment business, including movie stars, stage entertainers, sports figures and other people with high visibility

Jason added, "We hope we can also contribute to the decline of terrorism and kidnapping around the world. It's like the automobile Lojac system; thieves do not want to steal cars that can be instantly traced. Hopefully terrorist will not want to kidnap highly important people who just might have a Pinpoint, Inc. microchip in their body. We are confident our product will be a deterrent to some degree."

Jason then asked Jim Kraft, his technical director, to give an update on the company's satellite tracking system.

Jim took the floor. "As of today we are less than a week away from testing our system. The system will work along the same lines as a common GPS system used in cars and by companies to track locations of their vehicles. Ours, however, will have additional bio-medical capabilities to track, monitor and record body temperature. With this system we can record any change in body temperature that would reflect stress, sickness or even death. With this technique, we will always know if our client is alive and well."

Jason interjected, "Jim has done a great job in taking a tracking system that is on the market today and adapting new biomedical temperature reading techniques that will show us to be a leader in this field."

Jim continued, "We have researched the cost of our own satellite dish and the cost of leasing space on someone else's dish. Launching your own private dish is really expensive and not in our budget for now. Understanding that limitation, we researched the availability of other dishes. Our number one priority is to make sure our dish is reliable. You do not want a dish that might go in and out of operation due to weather conditions, location changes, bad maintenence or faulty materials. It is no surprise that lease pricing is based on how reliable the dish is and how much space is available on the dish. Of all the dishes available for lease, we think the dish used by Holiday Inn Hotels for their Holidex reservation system, is the most reliable. That company makes twenty seven million reservations each year and their system is well maintained and reliable. The day might come when we can afford our own dish, but for now, this is the best deal."

Jason next turned to Sid Worthington for a financial report.

Sid simply shook his head and said, "I don't know how you all do it, but we are pretty much on budget. You have been taking people to the finest restaurants, such as St. Elmo's Steak House downtown and Chanteclair, at the Holiday Inn at the airport and you're still staying within budget. You must be eating the Blue Plate Specials. Keep up the good work, and let's get this research and development period over and make some money."

Jason thought to himself, well, it wasn't the greatest report ever given, but what the hell, he's a financial guy and they are always boring! Hopefully he can add and subtract better than he can give interesting reports.

Jason asked for questions. Hearing none, he adjourned the meeting.

After walking around the office, thanking everyone for their hard work, Jason went to St. Elmo's for lunch. Although he never admitted it to himself, he did have a burning desire to get his social life back to normal. He was continually reminding himself about that ole saying, "all work and no play makes you think about sex all day," or something like that.

He was back in the hunt and scanning the room for female companionship. There were lots of middle-aged women in the room who ten years ago probably looked exactly like what he was looking for. There were also several younger women in the room that looked like neither of their parents ever won a beauty contest.

Of course his standards were high because he was always able to attract beauty along with the personality he wanted. Yes, he was picky and, because of that small character fault, lonely and sexually deficient. He would probably do what he always did, go back home and work on his company plans and maybe have a drink or two with his old buddies at the local bar. Other than work, his was a rather boring life.

At the next staff meeting Jason announced that he felt the company was ready to launch a marketing campaign and begin selling their product.

He went around the table and asked for everyone to give a status report on their responsibilities. Everyone was positive about being ready to market and sell.

Higgie said the microchip was ready to go. Jim Kraft said the tracking and the body heat mentoring systems were up and ready. John said the marketing and sales programs were ready. There wasn't much left to do but jump into action and establish the company and prove themselves.

"Ok then," Jason said. "Let's do it!" It was like smashing a bottle of champagne against the side of a newly built ship. Everyone applauded. Pinpoint, Inc. was officially launched.

CHAPTER SEVEN

MARKETING AND SALES

The entire management team worked on the development of a sales prospects list. Many lists were already available, whereas some had to be refined and developed. Some of the obvious ones were the US House of Representatives, the US Senate, the Joint Chiefs of Staff, White House personnel, the Secret Service, the CIA, the FBI, members of the Supreme Court, high-ranking government employees, ambassadors to foreign countries, governors, corporate executives, multi-millionaires, billionaires, entertainers, Hollywood stars, sports figures, mayors of major cities and anyone else who might be at risk for kidnapping and other terrorist acts.

While those lists were only in the United States, there were people in foreign countries that would be even more at risk than US citizens.

John Lewis spoke to Jason in his office, "My staff and I have put together various marketing tools that we think will have an impact on our potential clients. We have our entire story and the opportunities available for our clients on audiotapes, CD tapes, DVD disks and computer floppies. We also have it available in printed form including pamphlets, brochures and three ringed notebooks. Our web site, PinpointINC.com, is up and running.

Jason was impressed with the high quality of the material, even though he worked with John Lewis on all these sales tools.

"John, you're done a great job, where do you suggest we start first?" Jason said.

John replied, "I think the federal government will take some time because of all the red tape they have to go through to get something like this approved. It's not like a board of directors or company heads that can just approve the project. I suggest we send all forms of our information to the White House Chief of Staff as well as to the leadership of the Senate and House and ask for a meeting to discuss how we can assist in the security issues of our government leadership."

Jason thought for a moment and added, "In the meantime, we should spend our time approaching the business and entertainment industries. We could start with the Fortune 500 companies and major picture and recording studios. The word will get out."

Jason, Higgie and John Lewis went on the road promoting and selling Pinpoint, Inc. Surprisingly, they were well received and found that corporate leadership had bigger egos than they expected. Many corporate Founders, Chairmen, Presidents and CEO's they met considered themselves invaluable to their companies. Many had the impression, at least in their own minds, that their companies might collapse or go bankrupt if they were somehow removed from their positions.

Jason now considered corporate egos as the biggest selling tools they had. In some cases the Founder or CEO approved the project. Sometimes the company's board of directors approved the project. In some cases the board of directors insisted that the Founder or CEO have the chip implanted for the protection of the company. In other cases the chip was implanted even though the executive was not totally convinced that he or she should have the implant.

Jason was working hard and enjoying every minute. Sales

were good and the technical end of the business was well developed and working fine.

One typical call was to a company in New York City, a banking firm. Jason and Higgie made the sales call. They were to meet with a man named Samuel Rome, the President of the company.

The company was located in the 200 block of Park Ave., in Manhattan. The building was multi-story, modern, mostly glass and very impressive. Jason and Higgie took the elevator to the twenty-second floor. The office lobby looked like an art gallery with beautiful leather chairs and sofas. The receptionist sat behind a very expensive oversized mahogany desk and looked very official.

"Good morning, we have a ten o'clock appointment with Mr. Rome," Jason said. "My name is Jason Higgins and this is Miss Higginbothem." "Yes, Mr. Higgins, we were expecting you. Mr. Rome will be right with you. May I get you coffee, tea or a soft drink?" " No thank you," they both replied.

Ten minutes later, the receptionist guided Jason and Higgie to another reception area where a well-dressed woman in her forties sat behind still another large mahogany desk.

"Good morning, Mr. Higgins, I'm Lynn Pillow. Mr. Rome will see you now."

She led them into a very large corner office. Two walls were constructed of beautiful walnut panels while the other two walls were tinted glass. The carpet was thick and the office chuck full of art and antiques. And there, at one end of the office, in front of tinted glass windows, was still another, even larger, mahogany desk. Standing next to the desk was Mr. Samuel Rome.

Jason entered with his hand outstretched. Higgie trailed behind him.

"Good morning, Mr. Rome," Jason said. "My name is Jason

Higgins and this is Paula Higginbothem. Paula is our Director of Research."

"Good morning to you both and thank you for coming," Rome said in a clear, robust voice. "May I get you some coffee or perhaps a soft-drink?"

There was a slight hint of British English in the tone of his voice. He didn't seem to be British, but if not, he had certainly captured the British version of the English language.

Samuel Rome was a tall, stately, well-dressed, well-mannered gentleman. Higgie thought him to be one of the most handsome black men she had ever met. He was probably in is late fifties, had short gray hair, a thin gray mustache, was probably a little over six feet tall and weighed around 180 pounds. His skin was light for a black man and he seemed to be extremely competent and well educated.

Jason replied, "Not for me, Mr. Rome. Anything for you, Paula?"

"No thanks," she replied.

"Well then, have a seat," Mr. Rome asserted.

"Let's talk about your company first, and then we'll talk about my company."

Jason gave his patented speech. Leaning forward in his leather chair, he smiled and stared Samuel Rome straight in the eyes.

"First of all, thank you for allowing us to be here. We think we have a company that can be of great service to your company."

Jason tried to look and act relaxed and confident.

"We started our company two years ago. We know we have a solid concept. We have done our homework and are very confident about the quality of our product and services. There is no doubt that we have been very conscientious about our research and development. We know the value of our services and the responsibility we assume when we ask our clients for their business."

Leaning back in his chair Jason continued. "I know the material we sent you had a lot of information regarding our company and we hope you have had the time to review our company and the services we can provide."

"I read some of it," Samuel said with a grin.

"I didn't have time to go into great detail, so I had a few people here review the information and make a recommendation. We were impressed, so we passed the information on to our Board of Directors for review, along with a recommendation to 'seriously consider.'"

After a short pause Jason said, "Are there any questions I can answer or is there any part of our material that I can elaborate on in more detail?"

Samuel smiled back at Jason and said, "As I said, I was very impressed with your material and the way it was presented. I am even more impressed with the product you have developed and the comfort level you might provide our company. How did this idea start?"

Jason explained his background and his graduate school thesis. He explained how this technology could greatly enhance law enforcement efforts and could quickly resolve a serious criminal act before events could lead to a fateful conclusion. He also explained how the tracking systems work and how the heat sensor in the microchip could monitor the human body temperature and somewhat determine the condition of the body.

Samuel asked, "How is the microchip implanted and where?"

Higgie explained, "The position of the microchip is

optional. It is so small that it can be located anywhere in the human body."

Samuel grinned again and said, "How is it implanted? You see, some of us just look like rough, tough executives; down deep we're scared to death of needles, cutting skin and creepy things like that."

Higgie said, "Oh no, Mr. Rome, there is very little to be afraid of. We have a medical team that injects Novocain to the general area and after that, you don't feel a thing and it takes little time to insert the chip."

Jason asked, "Are you considering yourself as a candidate Mr. Rome? I was under the impression from our correspondence it was your chairman."

Samuel responded, "Well, our Board of Directors voted to have our chairman receive the chip. However, after that discussion, the decision was made that I too should have a chip. Neither of us had much choice in the matter. Of course that vote was contingent on our acceptance of the terms of the agreement."

Samuel continued, "You see we have very strict security standards. Our chairman and I are authorized to make extremely large transactions of millions and millions of dollars. We do it almost every day.

We need to agree on the initial and ongoing cost. We will then need a first-hand tour of your facilities in Indianapolis. When all that is complete, we will decide what our action will be. After that, I will give you a first hand tour of our financial transaction procedures. It is a very elaborate security-based system."

Jason said, "Do you understand the cost involved? If your company is going to have two people receive a chip, we can discount the initial cost."

Samuel replied, "Yes, I understand. As a matter of fact, I wanted to ask you if the cost would be different for two people."

Jason replied, "We would be happy to lower the initial cost from $125,000 apiece to $100,000 apiece. The ongoing monitoring cost would stay at $3000 per month each. As you know we do weekly checks on each microchip to make sure it is functioning properly. We also send a monthly report on the location of the microchip during one spot-check time. You, in turn, can verify that the chip is working properly because you will know where the person was at that time and can verify our report.

"I don't think the cost and ongoing expenses will be a problem," Samuel said.

They concluded the meeting with casual conversation about some Broadway shows. Jason told Samuel they wanted to attend a show that night, Chicago.

Samuel exclaimed, "Great show! You should see it tonight."

"Well, we'd love to, but getting tickets is very difficult," Jason replied.

Samuel stood up and grunted, "And you don't want to sit in the back of the theater. Give me a couple minutes." He left the office.

A few minutes later Samuel returned and said, "Lynn is working on something for you, give her a few minutes." After some more casual conversation Lynn came into the office and laid a piece of paper on Samuel's desk. He looked at it and said, "Wonderful, Lynn, thank you very much."

Samuel handed the paper to Jason and said, "Lynn has arranged for you to have two seats in the middle, second row. I may have to fire her for not getting you front row seats!"

Jason and Higgie laughed and Jason said, "Thank You, Mr. Rome, thank you very much. That was really kind of you. I have no idea how you did it, and maybe I don't need to know!"

"No, you don't want to know," He replied.

"I know, if you tell us, you'll have to kill us?" Jason quipped.

"That's right," Samuel said with another big grin.

Jason said, "Thank you very much for your time. We know you are busy and we appreciate the time you have given us. We'll look forward to hearing from you soon."

"It was my pleasure to meet you both. I'm sure we will see you in Indianapolis. We think your company will provide a great service to our company," Samuel replied.

They all shook hands and Lynn Pillow took them back to the main reception area. That night they had dinner at the LaPavillion, a very fine French restaurant, and attended "Chicago" They actually had a nice time together. It was all above board——-boss and employee, as it should be.

By the end of the first year of Pinpoint, Inc. the company had forty-two clients. The average initial cost for the microchip implantation and establishment of an account was $105,000. The average monthly monitoring cost was $3000 per account. They discounted the initial fee when necessary, but kept the monitoring fee at three thousand dollars.

Into the second year Jason had moved to a new home. There were no real love interests in his life, but he continued to be a part of the community and all the social circles available to an up-and-coming, good-looking man in his mid thirties.

His new home was on the west side of town, in a wooded area, with a large lake, called Eagle Creek. He had wanted to live on the northeast side, but Giest reservoir was located on that side of town and the negative memories were just too strong.

PINPOINT INC.

So, as Horace Greenly said, "Go west young man"; Jason went west.

The new house was a single-story, rustic, four-bedroom with a lot of open space. The house was three years old. It sat on a one-acre lot and was on one of the lake's inlets. Outside, he had a great patio overlooking the lake and a stone path to a boat dock. His twenty-two foot pontoon party boat was parked at his dock. From the street the house reminded one of a comfortable English cottage. It had lots of trees, bushes, flowers and landscaping. The garage was on the side of the house, so the look of the house sprawled across the landscape.

Life was good for Jason and the company. He was making good money. The company was paying its bills and more importantly, the second year brought seventy-three new clients for a total of one hundred and fifteen. The five-year plan was to have over 300 clients. That number could change quickly if the federal government increased the number of its clients, like all secret service or CIA agents. Some operatives in foreign countries were already clients, so the opportunities were there.

CHAPTER EIGHT

THE CALL

"Good morning, I'm Katie Couric. Welcome to the "Today Show", I'm here with Matt Lauer, Al Roker and Ann Currie. It's Tuesday, January seventeenth and we're here in New York on a cold and blustery day."

Katie, Matt and Al talked about the weather and preparations for Matt to travel around the world again on his Where in the world is Matt Lauer segments.

Then Matt said, "Now over to Ann Curry for the news. Ann, I hear you have an update on the local businessman who is missing."

"Yes I do Matt; and good morning to you, Katie, Al, and good morning, everyone."

After adjusting her papers in her hands, she said, "Last night in New York, local radio and television stations reported that the car of investment banker Harold Andrews was discovered in upstate New York, hidden under a brush pile. Authorities have now released information that the car did indeed belong to the Andrews International Banking Corporation. The car is believed to be Harold Andrews' personal car. He is the founder and owner of the company. Mr. Andrews reportedly drove from his home outside New York City to his lodge in the vicinity of Catskill, New York several days ago."

Turing to the other camera she continued, "Yesterday morning officials in Jasper, New York, discovered the car;

however, they did not release any information pending an investigation by state and federal authorities. Mr. Andrews' wife, in an interview last night at their home, indicated that Mr. Andrews often spent several days at his lodge, and that it was not unusual not to hear from him for extended periods of time."

Ann continued, "Mr. Andrews is the Founder and Chairman of a banking company responsible for millions of dollars of transactions each day among various oil producing countries around the world. The company is said to be the largest of its kind. Andrews International Investment Banking Corporation is privately owned and has never been on the New York or American stock exchanges. State and federal authorities have launched a search for the whereabouts of Mr. Andrews."

Ann reported some additional daily news and closed with, "And now back to you, Katie."

Katie closed the conversation on Harold Andrews, "Wow, that's really something. Mr. Andrews is a very wealthy and important businessman in this city; I hope he's ok."

Matt added, "I hope so, that's really is a big story. I'll bet the authorities will go 'all out' to find him quickly."

Before the Today Show was over, the phone rang at Pinpoint, Inc., in Indianapolis. The caller said, "Is Jason Higgins there, please?"

"Yes sir, just a second, sir."

"Hello, this is Jason Higgins."

"Jason, this is Samuel Rome, in New York. Have you heard the news this morning about our Chairman, Harold Andrews?"

"No Sir, I haven't heard any news this morning. We've been in a staff meeting since seven-thirty. What is the news? I hope everything is ok."

Samuel Rome replied, "No, Jason, it's not. Mr. Andrews

has disappeared and its looks like fowl play. We need to activate immediately."

Jason asked, "When did you find out?"

Samuel answered, "Well, I received a call late last night, but the authorities weren't sure how serious it was until this morning. I wanted to be sure before I called you."

Jason said, "We will have to go through our security procedures before we officially activate our search systems. When we do activate we will create a situation that will bring in federal authorities. We, of course, will launch our own investigation. First, I will have to call you back immediately to verify that you are making the call. I know you are Mr. Rome, but I need to play it by the book. This security system avoids any crank or unauthorized calls to activate."

"That's fine, Jason, I understand the procedures. Please call immediately. I am afraid this is a very serious situation and we have to move quickly."

Less than two minutes later, Jason was back on the phone with Samuel Rome. "Ok, Mr. Rome, as you know an emergency team has been pre-appointed by your company to coordinate all activities with your company. I will need to have a conference call with that group in thirty minutes. Please have the group assemble in your conference room as soon as possible. I would like to have you there.

Please be sure you have people to record every word and be prepared for members of your team to come to Indianapolis. I will make arrangements to come to your office and discuss the security risk for your company."

"Ok, Jason, I will be at the conference call in thirty minutes and will have our team ready.. Thirty minutes, Jason. My assistant, Lynn Pillow, will arrange the conference call and will call your office with the conference phone number for you to call. Thirty minutes!"

Jason thanked Samuel Rome and hung up the phone. He immediately contacted his systems technical director, Jim Kraft.

"Jim, this is Jason, We have a very serious situation. One of our clients has disappeared and he's a high visibility businessman."

"Who is it, Jason?" Jim asked with shock and concern.

"Harold Andrews in New York. He's the banker guy who handles all the money for the oil-producing countries, including all of OPEC." Jim paused. "Oh my god, I remember him. When did it happen?"

"I think it happened yesterday afternoon or evening, but the company wasn't officially notified until early this morning. I assume it was delayed because they had to verify the car and the owner. Maybe they weren't sure if fowl play was involved. At any rate, we need to move fast and pinpoint where Mr. Andrews is located. This is a terrible thing, but also a big break for us. This gives us a chance to show how good we are. It will be a great sales tool when we show how fast we located Harold Andrews."

Jim asked, "What do you want me to do first, Jason?"

"You need to locate him immediately. Notify the authorities and meet me in our conference room in fifteen minutes. We will have a conference call with their company team and give them the information on his location and where we go from there. Let's get going!"

"Right, Jason, see you in a few minutes."

Fifteen minutes later Jason and his team gathered in the conference room, ready to make the call to New York. Jim Kraft was not yet in the room.

Not to be late, Jason decided to make the call to Samuel

Rome even though Jim was not present. Jason dialed the conference call number. "Hello, this is Lynn Pillow."

"Hello, Ms. Pillow, this is Jason Higgins in Indianapolis."

"Hello, Mr. Higgins, our team is gathered and Mr. Rome will preside over the conference call from this end."

"Hello, Jason, we're all here," Samuel replied with a quick tone in is voice.

Jason thought it interesting that Samuel's voice did not sound as British as when they first met. In fact, it sounded more Brooklyn than British. Maybe under pressure he falls back to his native dialect.

"Good morning, everyone," said Jason. "We are currently waiting for Jim Kraft, our systems expert, to give us information on Mr. Andrews' current location and health. As soon as he has verified that information, he will contact federal authorities and report back to us."

Jason continued, "When we discover his location, we will want to develop a game plan for your company and Pinpoint, Inc. We will need to decide which local and state authorities to contact, who will keep in direct contact with them and how we can best work together. We have already asked Indiana Bell to establish a direct telephone and fax hookup between Jim Kraft's office and your office. You will need to provide us with a telephone number and a contact person to work with, Jim."

Jason continued, "In the event Mr. Andrews changes locations, we will need to immediately contact the authorities; however, I assume they will already have someone here working with Jim Kraft.

The door to the meeting room in Indianapolis opened quickly and Jim Kraft motioned for Jason to come out to the hallway.

Jason looked somewhat shocked, but said, "Excuse me, Mr.

Rome. I'm going to go check on Jim Kraft and I will be right back."

Jason quickly left the room and met a perplexed looking Jim Kraft in the hallway.

"What the hell is going on, Jim? Where is he?"

"God damn, Jason, you won't believe this, but he's in South Africa!

Not only is he in South Africa, but he's in the middle of nowhere! We have pinpointed him to a remote area in Kruger National Park, which is a lot of miles north of Johannesburg! On top of that, we don't think he's even in a game camp. We've checked the locations of the game camps and he's not within five miles of any of them. Hell, he must be taking a game ride or something. He keeps moving around a lot!"

"Oh, Jesus Christ!" Jason said with disgust. "What the hell are we going to tell Samuel Rome and the authorities?

Jim blurted out, "Shit, tell them the truth. What else can we do?"

"But, they're going to question if our system is working correctly!" Jason snapped back.

"Yea, so? Tell them we're sure that's where he is. We can't tell them how the hell he got there, but we can tell them the location. And I'm damn sure we're right!"

"Ok, let's go into to the meeting. Let me handle it," Jason replied.

When Jason and Jim returned to the meeting, Higgie was discussing with the team in New York how the tracking system worked. Some of the New York team were not involved with any of the technical discussions when the account was established.

"I'm back, Mr. Rome," Jason said with a voice he had to force to be calm and collected.

Jason held his voice steady, "I have some very disturbing

news regarding Mr. Andrews' current location. It seems that our system has him (there was a short pause before Jason could get it out of his mouth) in, of all places, South Africa."

All Jason could hear on the conference call was silence and then murmuring, whispering, and light chatter on the line.

Even the people in his boardroom had their mouths open in amazement.

"Mr. Rome, are you there?" asked Jason.

"Yes, Jason, I'm here, and I'm trying to make some sense out of what the hell you just said. It's very hard to believe it. I'm not saying your system doesn't work, but SOUTH AFRICA?"

"I know, Mr. Rome, it surprises me too. But facts are facts, and that's where he is. Do you have any idea why he would be South Africa? Do you have business there?"

Samuel replied, "We probably do. We handle transactions for a lot of countries who buy and sell oil. I think we have established accounts there and they probably have individual deposits with us for investment purposes. I do know we transfer money to South Africa from our permanent accounts from time to time."

Jason said, "Well, Mr. Rome, we need to have discussions with the authorities about all of this. I'm sure the authorities will be contacting you soon." He paused and then said, "I'm sorry, Mr.Rome, I know this is very difficult for you and your company. We will do everything we can to help get Mr. Andrews back safely. If it's any consolation, the implanted chip has confirmed that he is in good health. The microchip readings have indicated that his body temperature is not quite normal, but close to normal. We assume he is under a lot of stress."

Samuel said, "Thank you, Jason. That is good news. We should talk again today after we both talk to the authorities."

"Yes sir, Mr. Rome, we'll talk again later."

CHAPTER NINE

THE SEARCH

One hour after the conference call, two FBI agents arrived at the offices of Andrews Banking Co. in New York City. They approached the reception desk.

"Good morning, I am agent Donnelly and this is agent Henderson of the FBI. We are here to see Mr. Rome."

"One moment, please. I'll contact his office." She called Mr. Rome's office. Lynn Pillow answered.

"Yes, Ms Pillow, we have two FBI agents here to see Mr. Rome." After a brief pause on the phone the receptionist answered, "Yes, thank you, I will tell him."

She turned to the agents. "Mr. Rome will be with you shortly. He is on the phone."

Agent Pete Donnelly answered, "Thank you. We'll wait."

"Can I get you anything?" the receptionist asked.

Donnelly looked at Henderson, "Anything for you, Jane?"

"Well, I could use a restroom."

The receptionist pointed down the hall. "Just go down this hall. The lady's is the second door on the left."

As agent Henderson was leaving Pete Donnelly replied, "Nothing for me, thanks."

Ten minutes later Lynn Pillow came to the reception area. "Hello, I'm Lynn Pillow, Mr. Rome's assistant. He will see you now." She led them back to Mr. Rome's office, knocking on the door as she opened it.

Pete Donnelly thought it strange that Lynn Pillow just knocked and opened the door without saying a word to Mr. Rome. They must have a close working relationship.

Samuel rose from his desk and walked around to shake hands with the two agents. "Thank you for coming. I'm Samuel Rome."

"Yes sir, I'm agent Pete Donnelly and this is agent Jane Henderson." They all sat in a cluster of chairs in the middle of the room.

Pete continued, "Mr. Rome, when did you first find out that Mr. Andrews was missing or, should I say, that his car had been discovered?"

"Well, the local authorities called me at home last night to tell me that the car had been discovered around seven p.m."

"And you waited until today to call state and federal authorities?" Pete replied.

"Why yes, the local authorities only told me that they had discovered a car belonging to Mr. Andrews. They did not say he was in danger. I was told an investigation would begin immediately and that they would contact me today. I assumed they would contact other authorities."

"And then what happened?" asked Jane.

"About seven-thirty this morning I received another call saying that Mr. Andrews had not been found and that they suspected fowl play because the car was purposely hidden and had bullet holes."

"What did you do after you received that call?" asked Jane

"I called my board of directors together for a conference call and told them what I knew."

"And what time was that call?" she asked again.

"The conference call was set up for 8:15 a.m."

"Were all the board members present for the call?" asked Pete.

"All except one. He was on a cruise ship and could not be reached at the time. We will continue trying to reach him today."

"Could you give us his name and contact information?" Pete asked.

"Of course, my assistant Ms. Pillow will have it for you when you leave."

"Do you know of anyone who might want to harm or kidnap Mr. Andrews, either for ransom or revenge?" Jane asked. "We assume you have not been contacted by anyone in regards to Mr. Andrews?"

"No, No, I have not been contacted," Samuel replied in a sharp, nervous manner. "I would certainly tell the authorities if I had been contacted. Why would I not tell the authorities?"

Pete assured Samuel that the question was not meant to imply that he might keep information from the authorities; it was just a routine question that had to be asked.

"Mr. Andrews is the founder and chairman of this company?" Pete asked.

"Yes, Yes," Samuel replied. "Mr. Andrews founded the company several years ago. I am the President and CEO and Mr. Andrews is the Chairman of the Board."

Pete continued, "Is Mr. Andrews here every day?"

"No," Samuel replied. He comes in for scheduled meetings and when major transfers of funds are made. He's not here every day, but is here most of the time, and often, for many days at a time."

"Is it important that he be here or does he just run board meetings?" Jane asked.

Samuel replied, "Yes, it is important that he be here most of the time because he is authorized to make major money transfers on behalf of our clients. If anyone else makes transfers, besides myself or Mr. Andrews, there are limits and strict rules."

"Why do you need him if you can make the transfers?" asked Pete.

"I can authorize transfers up to fifteen million dollars, but larger transfers can only be made by Mr. Andrews. Several other corporate officerscan approve five million dollar transfers, but Mr. Andrews has no limit. He keeps a pretty tight reign on the security of the transfers. If Mr. Andrews is not available and a large transfer needs to be made, there are various combinations of officers who can make the transfer, but it's somewhat complicated. It's just a lot easier if Mr. Andrews is here."

"Each transaction has a series of security actions in order to transfer the funds. We have a computer security system that only allows the transaction based on human handprints and fingerprints. Without the correct hand and finger print, the transaction won't go through. In some cases it requires an eye retina reading."

Samuel continued, "For example, a transfer over fifteen million dollars requires Mr. Andrews, and if he is not available, and the amount is over our combined limits, it takes the entire board of directors. I know it sounds very restrictive, but again, I say, it's intended to be."

Pete looked at Samuel with some amazement and said, "I'm not sure I understand what your company does. I thought it was just a matter of clients depositing and withdrawing funds. But now it sounds a little more complicated than that."

"It's a lot more complicated than that. We do not have a lot of clients, but the ones we have transfer huge sums of money every day. Most of our clients are foreign countries that produce oil. These are countries that have a lot of revenue available to them, but little infrastructure, or banking systems within their countries that are secure. They use us to hold and transfer most of their oil producing revenues between countries and corporate accounts. We also act as a clearinghouse for funds that are invested and waiting to be transferred later. Most countries feel we can provide the security shield from internal fraud and corruption within their own borders."

"My God," Pete said, "I had no idea that money like that moved around so easily each day. I knew that New York was an international investment haven. However, I never thought about these types of countries trusting the American system, since they do not have good things to say about us publicly. How many countries like this do you have as clients?"

"We have most of the oil producing countries and many other countries that do business with them. The countries that don't produce oil, buy oil. So, we are the financial connection between countries buying and selling. When a purchase is made, the funds come to us and are deposited in the oil producing company's master accounts. Those funds are invested in the best possible revenue producing portfolios and when the oil producing company wants their money, we transfer it to them or to another account as they direct."

"Who are your primary clients?" Pete asked.

"Well, the OPEC countries would be our primary clients."

"All the OPEC countries?" Pete quizzed.

"Yes. The largest OPEC clients are Indonesia, Saudi Arabia, United Arab Emirates and Venezuela. However, all are clients."

Pete said, "Jason Higgins and I are leaving for South Africa tomorrow. We have already notified local authorities in Johannesburg and they are arranging all the manpower we will need to search an area adjacent to Kruger National Park. Before we depart tomorrow night from Atlanta, we will meet with Jason in Indianapolis and review their systems. Agent Henderson will stay in Indianapolis to help supervise at Pinpoint, Inc. Also, we will establish a direct phone and fax line between their office and police offices in Johannesburg. We will need to stay in constant contact during the search. That will be done with a wireless communications systems linked to the phone line."

"Will you keep us informed?" asked Samuel.

Pete answered, "Someone from our office or the federal marshall's office here in New York will keep you informed, and if we need any assistance, agent Henderson will contact you."

Pete looked at Samuel. "Is there anything else we need to know?"

"Do you have all the information and descriptions on Mr. Andrews?" Samuel replied.

"Yes, we have various pictures, descriptions, fingerprints and dental charts. If we need anything else, we will contact you."

"Do we know how to get in contact with you if we are contacted or have additional information?" asked Samuel.

"We will leave all that information with your assistant," Jane answered.

Samuel stared across the room and through one of his large windows. "I can't believe this has actually happened. We all know the world is full of evil, but you really never focus on it until it hits you at home. Please do everything you can and bring Mr. Andrews back to us."

Pete thought to himself that the sentiment was nice, but the sound and tone of his voice was as if he's being melodramatic and insincere. It was almost as if he had already thought about what he would say before we came to his office.

Pete and Jane thanked Samuel for his time and left his office.

That evening they were at LaGuardia Airport and on their way to Indianapolis. They would arrive and stay at the Holiday

Inn at the airport. The next morning they would rent a car, drive to the FBI office in Indianapolis, have lunch and then drive to Pinpoint Inc. The staff at Pinpoint Inc. would brief them and the next day Pete and Jason would fly to Atlanta for their evening flight to Johannesburg.

The next day Pete and Jane were at the reception desk in Jason's office in north Indianapolis.

"Good morning, my name is Pete Donnelly and this is agent Jane Henderson. We are from the FBI and have an appointment with Jason Higgins."

"Of course, we were expecting you," replied the receptionist.

"Please wait right here and I will see if Mr. Higgins is available."

She returned in three minutes. "He will be right with you. He is with Jim Kraft, our technical director."

"Thank you," Pete answered.

They waited for five minutes and Jason appeared at the door.

"I'm very sorry to keep you waiting. We've had some interesting events this morning that I will need to discuss with you." He then paused and said, "Oh, I'm sorry, I'm Jason Higgins."

"Hello, Mr. Higgins. I'm Pete Donnelly and this is agent Jane Henderson. I'm sure these are some difficult times for you."

Jason said, "Yes, thanks, we have some interesting news to give you. Why don't you both come with me. I want you to meet Jim Kraft, our technical director. He's in the computer tracking room."

They all came into the tracking room to find Jim Kraft

typing furiously on the keyboard of a very large computer system. The room almost looked the inside of Starship Enterprise.

Jim stopped typing and stood up.

"Jim, these are agents Donnelly and Henderson from the FBI. The agency has assigned them to the Andrews case." They all shook hands.

Jason invited Pete and Jane to sit facing the computer tracking system so Jim could explain how it worked and what information it provided.

Jim explained, "I assume you know about our business and our microchip?"

Pete and Jane shook their heads yes. Jane asked, "After the chip is imbedded, how does it work?"

Jim stood and walked to the 50-inch video screen located on a shelf just above a series of keyboards. "Our computer systems are programmed to identify the microchips we have activated. Each microchip has its own identification. When the ID codes are put into the computer tracking system, the satellite system will show the exact location in longitude and latitude. The computer system will automatically convert that location and reflect it on our video screen.

The first conversion will show the location on a worldwide mapping system. We can then convert the visual display down to a country, a region, or a city and finally pinpoint a location down to a square city block area."

Jim moved closer to the computer, pointed to the video screen and continued, "The system resets itself every five minutes, so we are able to detect movement in five-minute intervals."

Pete and Jane listened with interest and thought about the value of this system to law enforcement. Jane asked, "So if there is movement, that obviously means the victim in still alive."

Jim answered, "Well, the victim could be dead and taken

somewhere in a vehicle or even carried. However, we have another method to determine that fact. The microchip can also detect and monitor body temperature in five-minute intervals showing the physical and medical condition of our client. Body temperature can change slightly with increased and decreased weather conditions. So, for example, we might be able to tell if our client is in a hot or cold climate."

Jim continued with a sense of accomplishment. "We might also predict our client's life expectancy by declining temperature stages. There are other reasons the body temperature might change, like sickness. All in all, we can keep a pretty close tab on our clients."

Pete looked a Jason and said, "Well, it looks like you will be able to give us a lot of assistance when we get to South Africa. We will station agent Henderson here at your company to help Mr. Kraft and the others. She and Jim will be our main contacts to inform us on his location and condition."

Jason replied, "We know Mr. Andrews is alive and well because he has moved one mile since last night. He is now northeast of his location yesterday evening. His body temperature is slightly elevated and that might be because the nights in South Africa are very cool, or he may always have an elevated body temperature. That's something we need to check with his doctor."

Pete asked, "Will Pinpoint, Inc. have direct contact with us at all times? We were told that a wireless communication system would be in place. I assume we will use cell phones."

"Our company will have an open line to us at all times," Jason said. "We also have an additional check point. I happen to have a microchip in me and we have activated my chip. This will tell Jim Kraft where we are compared to Mr. Andrews. He can tell us if we are getting close and when we hit the target."

"Great!" Pete replied, "We better get out of here and get to the airport. We will fly to Atlanta and on to Johannesburg tonight. It's about a fourteen or fifteen hour flight. We can contact agent Henderson and Mr. Kraft as soon as we get there. You can take us to the airport, then. Agent Henderson will have our car here. All my arrangements have been made. Let's go," Jason said.

They left Jane Henderson and Jim Kraft in the tracking room and headed for Jason's car.

CHAPTER TEN

SOUTH AFRICA

Jason and Pete left on Delta flight #7800, also known as South African Airways flight # 212. It was the same plane, a South African Airways plane, but Delta is a partner airline, so Delta sells it. They left at 6:30 pm and arrived in Johannesburg at 3:40 pm the next day. They flew business class, but only because the airline upgraded their tickets when they found out Pete was FBI. Actually Pete said they were both agents and showed his credentials upon check-in. They didn't ask for Jason's credentials, so both were upgraded. The flight was fifteen hours and ten minutes and they traveled 8439 miles.

It was a long, but comfortable flight. They read, watched a movie, ate dinner and still got several hours sleep. Pete said to Jason; "This is much better than flying to Europe. Those flights are around seven or eight hours and by the time you eat, see a movie and try to sleep, the damn plane is landing and you're dead tired."

The flight was met by a young woman from "The Conservation Corporation frica." This is an organization of game camps, lodges and hotels dedicated, as they say, "to offer you an Africa of vast, wild spaces and unparalleled luxury, embraced by a commitment to care for the land, wildlife and people."

Pete, being a federal agent of the United States, would be hosted at Londolozi, a luxury camp owned and operated by

Conservation Corporation Africa. Jason would be hosted the same camp, but Pete was the VIP because he was a US Federal Agent.

When they departed the plane, at the Johannesburg airport, Addie Smith, agent for the Conservation Corporation Africa, met them in the luggage area. Everyone introduced themselves.

"Welcome to South Africa," Addie cheerfully acclaimed. "We are happy you're here and we're looking forward to hosting you during your stay. You're scheduled to depart this airport at seven thirty tomorrow morning for Skukuza Airport, in the Sabi Sand Game Reserve, bordering the Kruger National Park, Mpumalanga Province. From there you will be transported, by our rangers, in an open vehicle to Londolozi, our private game reserve. I understand you have business in Kruger National Park, which is adjacent to Londolozi and separated only by the Sand River."

Addie continued while she had porters gather their luggage. "I know you are probably tired from your long flight, so we have arranged for you to stay at the Santon Sun-Intercontinental Hotel, not far from the airport. Adjacent to the hotel is our largest indoor shopping center and several very good restaurants. We will pick you up at six o'clock tomorrow morning and transport you to the airport. Is there anything else I can do for you?"

Pete answered, "Addie, thank you for our arrangements. Yes, there is something you can do. We need to get in touch with the American Embassy and our FBI counterpart here in Johannesburg. Maybe I should do That now, before we depart for the hotel. It's late in the afternoon, and I don't want to keep them too long at their offices."

Addie said, "Of course, I will take you both to our lounge here at the airport and you can use our phone."

"That would be great," Jason replied.

Addie escorted Pete and Jason to the lounge, offered them soft drinks and excused herself to check on the luggage and transportation.

Pete called his local FBI contact first.

He dialed the phone number and a man answered, "Hello, Laurie Mann, may I help you."

"Hello, yes Laurie, this is Pete Donnelly, we talked yesterday."

"Yes, Yes, Mr. Donnelly, welcome to South Africa. We are so happy to have you here, even under these cloudy circumstances. We have made all the arrangements for you. As you know we have been working with the Conservation Corporation Africa and they will take good care of you. I understand you will stay tonight in Sandton and tomorrow we will fly to the Skukuza airport. It's very close to Kruger National Park. I will go with you."

Pete responded, "Thanks, we have been met here at the airport by a lovely young lady named Addie Smith, and she has briefed us on our plans for tonight and tomorrow morning."

"Lovely," Laurie replied. "She is very competent and will take good care of you. Can we have dinner tonight and discuss my plans to assist you on your mission?"

Pete answered, "Of course, that would be wonderful. We need your help. We have a difficult job ahead of us."

"Ok then, I will pick you up at seven-thirty at your hotel, the Sandton Sun. Is Mr. Higgins with you?"

"Yes, he is here and we are looking forward to meeting you."

"Wonderful, you can dress casual and I will see you both at seven-thirty."

Before hanging up, Laurie added, "I think the American

Embassy is expecting a call from you, just to stay involved in your mission here."

"I intend to call their office as soon as we hang up," Pete answered.

Laurie replied with a cheerful voice, "Ok then, I will see you at seven-thirty."

Pete dialed the American Consulate General Office in Johannesburg. The main Embassy office is in Pretoria, the Capital. However, they have other offices in the country.

"Hello, this is the American Consulate General office," the voice on the other end of the line said.

"Hello, this is FBI agent Pete Donnelly. I would like to speak to the Consulate General please."

"Yes, Mr. Donnelly, one moment please."

After a short pause a strong, low voice said, "Hello, this is Timothy Stringfellow."

"Good afternoon Mr. Stringfellow, this is FBI agent Pete Donnelly."

"Hello, Mr. Donnelly, welcome to Johannesburg, I was expecting your call. We are pleased to have you in our country. I understand we have a situation in one of our parks up north. You will be looking for an American citizen?"

"Yes sir," Pete answered. "He is a very prominent American citizen. He has disappeared from the United States and we believe he is located in the Kruger National Park area."

"Yes, I understand it's Harold Andrews of New York. I have heard of him," Stringfellow commented.

Pete said, "We will be working with Laurie Mann of our FBI office here in Johannesburg. I have already contacted him and we will meet tonight to discuss our plans."

Stringfellow stated, "Yes, Laurie Mann, a very good person.

Do you need any assistance from our office? Mr. Andrews seems to be a very important businessman. We have direct instructions from our office in Washington D.C. to lend any assistance possible."

"Well, we may, Mr. Stringfellow. I think that, for now, our agent here has arranged the manpower and equipment we'll need. If we need any help in dealing with the South African government, we may call on your office."

"Please do so, Mr. Donnelly. We are anxious to get this situation resolved. Our office does wish to cooperate."

Pete added, "We will have direct wireless communications between our FBI office here in Johannesburg and our offices in the Untied States, including a company in Indianapolis who is working with us. All will have cell-phone contact with us in the field."

After Pete let all that information sink in, he added, "If your office needs to contact us, you can do so through our FBI agent Laurie Mann's office."

"Yes, well then, best of luck in your hunt, Mr. Donnelly. I hope you find your man. I understand the FBI always finds their man."

"Thank You, Mr. Stringfellow, we will stay in contact."

Pete turned to Jason and said, "I think that covers all bases. We will have dinner with Laurie Mann tonight, make final arrangements, and start our hunt tomorrow. If we need the US Embassy, I think we have the Consulate General in our back pocket."

Jason then made an International call to Indianapolis just to let everyone there know that he and agent Donnelly had arrived safely.

He told Jane Henderson and Jim Kraft that as soon as

they arrived in Kruger National Park they would contact them again.

They waited for Addie Smith to return and off they went to the Sandton Sun Hotel.

When they arrived at the hotel, they were surprised to find it in the middle of several large building complexes. Attached to the hotel, by a connecting walkway, was a huge three-story indoor shopping mall. The complex looked like a typical mall in the United States with most of the stores being upscale by American standards.

At the entrance of the Santon Sun Intercontinental Hotel was a very large three-story lobby. The lobby had several shops and a lounge bar. The floor was marble and the walls were mostly glass and marble. It was decorated well, but still seemed a little stark. Maybe it was the high ceilings.

Addie took Pete and Jason straight to the concierge desk for check-in.

Addie said, "We will meet you here in the lobby tomorrow at six a.m. If you want breakfast, you should eat before then. We will have coffee and rolls for you during the ride to the airport and on the plane. The plane is a twin-engine, twelve-passenger craft. I will accompany you, along with your agent here in Jo-berg, Laurie Mann."

Pete smiled, "Thank you, Addie. We'll look forward to seeing you bright and early in the morning."

When Addie left, Pete looked at Jason and said, "Jo-berg, that's a lot easier to say. I'll remember that."

They went to their rooms and got ready for dinner. There was no reason to unpack; it was a one-night stand. The rooms were typical to an upscale hotel room in the States, maybe a little larger.

At 7:15 Pete and Jason met in the lobby. They had discussed

meeting earlier for a drink, but decided there was too little time. They needed time to freshen up.

Laurie Mann met them in the hotel lobby at 7:30.

They walked from the lobby to an exit that connected the hotel to the shopping mall next door. As they walked through the mall, Jason noticed many pieces of African art and upscale stores.

Jason stopped at one of the storefronts and said, "Pete, look at all these beautiful hand carved statues of elephants, lions, giraffe, and other African wildlife. And, the prices are reasonable."

Pete stopped at another store window and commented, "My god, look at the beautiful hand-made African rugs, every color in the rainbow! And that one there, it's a zebra skin rug. I bet that costs a fortune."

They continued through the mall. Jason commented, "I've never seen so much hand-made jewelry. Look at the wooden mask and weapons. The color and craftsmanship are superb!"

Jason had visions of coming back to the mall before they left South Africa.

They continued their walk to the restaurant as they passed Jewelry stores that sold diamonds, precious stones, custom jewelry and watches such as Rolex and Seiko.

When they reached the restaurant, Laurie said, "This is it. I hope you like it. It's one of the better restaurants in town."

Jason noticed that even though the restaurant décor was rustic, it was also upscale. "Pete, look at the ceiling. Good lord, it's all hand—carved wood."

Pete looked and replied, "I wouldn't want the job of carving that. Whoever did it must have had a damn sharp carving knife or whatever tool they use for that type of work."

They were both impressed with all the artifacts in the room. The receptionist led them through two rooms into a large room that had a beautiful window view of a running waterfall against the back wall.

Laurie said, "I hope this is ok, it's a beautiful room."

"This is very impressive," Jason answered.

They ordered wine and reviewed the menu.

Laurie said, "Do you have anything in particular in mind? If not, I would recommend the grilled Royal Tiger Prawns. They're the best in town."

"Sounds good to me," Pete replied. "I always say, when in Rome, shoot a roman candle, or something like that." They all laughed.

After ordering, Pete asked Laurie, "Tell us about the arrangements you have made. I know from our phone call the other day that you understand our mission."

Laurie briefed them on the arrangements. "When we arrive at the Londolozi Game reserve we will have four game-viewing vehicles to take us to the area that your office has identified. Each vehicle will have a game reserve ranger, a local tracker and one of us. The rangers and the trackers are employees of the Londolozi reserve. The rangers will drive the vehicles and carry rifles for our protection from the animals or whatever else we may need protection from. The trackers are native Africans who can track and spot animals that have not even been in the area for hours. They are unbelievable in their tracking abilities."

Jason asked Laurie, "What do you suggest we do when we reach the game preserve? How much time will we have?"

"Well, the first thing you should do is check in with your company in Indianapolis and verify the correct location. I understand from Jason that your last contact yesterday showed the location one and one-third miles to the northeast from where it was the day before.

Jason said, "We are fortunate to have a microchip inside me. We will be able to be guided by my office in Indianapolis and they will be able to see my chip and Mr. Andrews' chip at the same time. Obviously, their job is to bring the two chips together. All we have to do is keep in contact with our wireless phone, and when the microchips merge, we will find Mr. Andrews."

"What do we do if the capturers are armed?" Laurie said.

Pete answered, "Laruie, I don't want to get anyone hurt and we don't know if he has been captured or is working on his own. We need to have a briefing with the rangers and trackers about that risk. It will be up to you, Jason and me to take care of whatever situation we find ourselves in. Jason and I are still a little confused by the whole situation. We still don't understand why Mr. Andrews would be in a South African Game Reserve. If he is being held against his will, it's a strange and very dangerous place to be."

Jason looked at Pete with some alarm. "What the hell do you mean by "us" taking care of whatever situation we may be in? I'm not trained to shoot or capture people. Hell, I don't even have a gun!"

Pete laughed. "You will have one by tomorrow and tomorrow you will "almost" be an unofficial FBI agent."

"I don't like the way you said almost and unofficial," Jason retorted. "This is your job, to get Mr. Andrews safely home."

"Yes, and it's your ass on the line if something goes wrong and we don't find Mr. Andrews. Isn't it your company that says they know where he is at all times? Besides, all you have to do is point the damn thing, squeeze the trigger, and presto, you're a gun-slinging FBI agent..... almost!

Jason looked at Pete with an expression that said, "You've got to be kidding." Then he grinned and said, "Does this mean I get one of those big government pensions?"

"I....don't....think....so," Pete said in a slow, drawn-out tone.

Laurie laughed. "You guys are a great team and very funny. However, my thought was to arrive at the edge of the area, have the vehicles and trackers drive slowly about forty or fifty yards apart. We should be able to over a fairly large area quickly, especially if the microchip can really be detected within a city block area."

"That sounds good to me," Pete replied. Turning to Jason with a smile he asked, "What do you think, Agent J?"

Jason replied, "I don't want to get killed and neither do the trackers, so what are we going to tell them to do when we see Mr. Andrews and whoever is with him?"

Pete answered, "I think that as soon as visual contact is made, the rangers and trackers should retreat to our rear for backup." Jason asked, "What the hell does that mean? We're getting out of the vehicles on foot and they take the vehicles? Why can't I just go with them and you and Laurie capture the bad guys?"

"No, you're staying with us, and they can get out and walk to the rear. Hell, Jason, they walk and live among killer animals all day, I would imagine they have faced a little danger now and then! I think it's a great idea to have them watch our asses."

Jason frowned, but agreed.

They had dinner and returned to the hotel. Pete and Jason thanked Laurie, confirmed the plans for the next morning, and went to their separate rooms.

At 5:00 a.m. Jason's alarm went off. He had not slept well

because of the time difference between Indianapolis and South Africa. He woke up a couple times during the night and thought about the plans for the next day. All in all he was still tired. He knew that his lack of sleep was from worrying about becoming an unofficial FBI agent.

Pete woke at 5:05a.m. The room had a four-cup coffee maker with only one pack of coffee. He thought to himself, when are these damn hotels going to wake up and realize that one coffee pack is not enough coffee to make four cups? All it does is get you get damn weak coffee. This was not building a great mood to start the day.

They met Addie and Laurie in the hotel lobby at 6:05 a.m. Pete blamed the tardiness on weak coffee and the lack of caffeine.

They arrived at the airport at 6:45 a.m. and went directly to the terminal for Million Air, a charter air company. After some real coffee and breakfast rolls, they reviewed their plans with Laurie.

At 7:15 a.m. they boarded the twelve-passenger, twin-engine plane. They were instructed to sit in particular seats in order to balance the weight of the passengers. Their baggage was weighed to insure that the pilot had the correct weight for the entire aircraft.

A loud roar from the engines made conversation difficult as they taxied from the parking area and headed towards the runway. The taxi seemed forever, but understandable, since the charter companies are farther from the main terminals and the runways.

Jason commented, "Lord, are we driving to Londolozi or are we actually going to get into the air at some point?" It sounded rather funny, but they were all ready to get to their destination.

Pete and Jason sat in row three. Laurie and Addie sat across the isle, two rows behind, over the wing, next to the engines. It was very loud all the way.

Forty minutes later the plane circled the Skukaza airport, bordering Kruger National Park.

The view from the air was beautiful. Looking closely, they could see a few animals wondering through the bush. The bush in the northern part of South African was different than the ones in Kenya, the Rift Valley and the Serengeti plains in East Africa. In South Africa there were small hills and valleys and the vegetation was taller and closer together. Although the land was sandy, the umbrella shaped trees and underbrush were in clusters the size of a city block, with open spaces and small bushes between. In this area, on the ground, they could see about one block in front because of the bushes and trees. They could accidentally drive right up to an animal before actually seeing it. This was unlike Kenya, in central Africa, where you could go miles before seeing a stand of trees or underbrush.

"There are two elephants!" Jason exclaimed. Pete and Jason both leaned closer to the window of the plane to get better views.

Pete turned around and asked Addie, "Are the animals enclosed in a certain area?"

"Most of the private reserves do have fences, but the areas are so vast that many of the larger animals, like elephants, just push the fences down and go wherever they want to go. Many of the other animals just go over or under the fences. The only real reason for the fences is to identify the reserve's borders."

As the plane landed, it bobbed and weaved from left to right and hovered just off the runway. There didn't seem to be very much wind. It was just the way the plane responded when landing. No big deal for the locals, but Pete and Jason's stomachs fluttered a bit.

As the plane taxied toward a small building that was the terminal, Jason could see two large open jeeps parked next to the terminal. Next to the jeeps were four young, white men in ranger uniforms.

Laurie and Addie were the first to depart the plane. They walked towards the rangers and shook hands. Pete and Jason followed and were introduced to the four rangers.

"Which Jeep do you want us in?" Pete asked one of the rangers.

"This one would be fine, sir," he replied, in a polite, slightly British accent. "We will take the four of you in this one and we will use the other Land Rover for the luggage."

Pete said, "Oh, they're Land Rovers. That's an expensive vehicle."

The ranger replied, "Most of the camps have land rovers. They last a long time and they'll go anywhere. When you do what we do, you sometimes need to get out of where you are in a hurry."

"I guess you're right," Jason added.

As they pulled away from the airport they noticed that there were no paved roads. All the roads were dirt with only the tire track area actually packed. They were bumpy and hard. The Land Rovers were dependable, but obviously not built for comfort. On the dashboard were quick release fasteners that held a fairly large, bolt-action rifle. The rifle that looked like it could take down an elephant or rhino. The question Jason asked himself was; how fast can the ranger get the damn rifle out of the fasteners? He thought to himself; "hopefully before the animal can get to the ranger, or more importantly, to me."

The ride to Londolozi took about 30 minutes. They saw zebras, giraffes, warthogs and gazelles along the way. Their driver said; "You would think you are in a zoo, but this is real. Our animals are living on their land, in their territory. When you visit here, keep in mind that if you make a mistake you may die. If you die, it's not the animals' fault.

Londolozi's main camp has eight double en-suite chalets and two luxurious granite suites. It is self-contained with its own boma, pool, leisure deck, bar and lounge area overlooking the Sand River.

Jason was interested in the term Boma. Turning to Addie he asked, "What is a boma? I've heard of it, but I'm not quite sure what one is."

Addie explained, "In simple terms, it is a large walled area outside the living areas that protect the people from wild animals when they are outside for a gathering. The walls are about 8-10 feet high, usually made from natural wood and bark strips. The entry is built in a spiral manner for the first thirty feet to deter any animal from entering the main gate or opening. The entry looks like a curved hallway for that first 30 feet. We will have dinner

inside the boma tonight. A typical boma will hold a hundred or more people at a gathering."

Knowing that time was important, Pete told the group, "I would like to tour the facility and learn more about the area, but we are on a tight schedule and people's lives are in the balance. We need to find Mr. Andrews and get him home. Let's get something to eat and start the search this afternoon."

With that, Addie excused herself and headed for the dining room.

Laurie, Pete and Jason went to the reception desk and

checked in. Attendants took their luggage to their assigned chalet and they went to the dining room.

Just after lunch, Jason contacted Indianapolis. Jane Henderson and Jim Kraft were waiting for the call.

"Hello Jim, this is Jason."

Jim replied, "We've been waiting for your call. We have some more news for you."

"I hope it's good news."

"Well, we're not sure. We're surprised that Mr. Andrews seems to be moving around the area again. He has moved almost half a mile since last night. His vital signs seem to be ok, but we can't figure out why he keeps moving around so much. If he's walking, that's a hell of a walk."

Jason relayed the information to Pete.

"Would his capturers know that he has a microchip inside him?" Pete asked.

"If they did their homework they might. There are no physical signs on his body that would show where a chip was planted. Then again, they may have made him tell."

"Ok, Jim, where is he now?" Jason asked.

"He's a half mile north/northeast of his location last night."

"OK, our rangers can figure that out. We will keep our wireless communications open. You're tracking the chip in me, aren't you? As we get closer, you can guide my chip directly to Mr. Andrews' chip."

"We will keep you going in the right direction," Jim said.

"Right. Talk to you later."

Laurie assembled the rangers and trackers. Pete gave a detailed briefing of what their mission was. They all moved to the land rovers in the parking area.

For the drive to the staging area a ranger drove, and Laurie,

Pete and Jason rode in the rear seats. The drive would take about forty-five minutes. They would have to go slightly out of the way to cross the Sand River.

Each of the other three Land Rovers had a ranger and trackers. They circled out of the parking area and headed north/northeast into the bush. Jason was preoccupied with the handgun hanging on his belt that Pete had given him. He turned to Pete and said, "If this damn thing goes off before we get there, I'm suing the government."

Pete, bouncing around in his seat, said, "If that gun goes off and it's pointed down towards your butt, you'll either have a really sore ass or a hole in your leg. If that happens, you'll be begging us to take you back to a hospital. Unless you drop the lawsuit, I won't take you. Any questions?"

"No questions," Jason grinned.

The road consisted of lumps of dirt and gravel with tire ruts and signs of erosion. Even the best shock absorbers couldn't make these roads smooth and it felt like these Land Rovers had no shocks.

They were less than a mile away when a herd of impala came into view less than a block away. There were over a hundred in the herd. Some jumped and ran and some continued grazing. They did seem a little jumpy and the guide said they are known as breakfast, lunch and dinner in the African bush land. A lot of larger, faster animals love to eat impala. It is the food of choice in the bush.

Jason turned again to Pete and said, "You know, when all of this is over, we might need to come back here and really enjoy this place."

"Oh sure," Pete muttered. "You know what kind of money FBI agents make? I'll bet the nightly rate here is about what

I make in a week and that's not counting airline cost. Hell, my business class ticket says $6,400! If you're thinking about coming back, Mr. big time company president, and you want me to come with you, it would be on your dime, which means I probably won't be coming back!"

They both grinned. Jason thought to himself that it was kind of fun being friends with a FBI agent.

As they approached the Sand River crossing, the guide pointed out several hippos in the river. He told them how the hippo's ears open and close when they submerge in water and the fact that they can stay under for several minutes. "Surprisingly, hippos kill more humans than most other animals in South Africa because they panic when they feel threatened. You do not want to get between a hippo and his water and have him panic. He will run you down. They do not eat people, but when threatened it will take a human in its mouth and take him under water and drown him. Being eaten would be your second worry."

Once across the river, the group passed into Kruger National Park.

They had received permission from the government to enter. However, game lodge rangers did not have any control over the park. They were to report to the park rangers if they intended to spend any long period of time in the park. As they continued over very bumpy roads, they continued to see impalas. They were everywhere, always ready to be lunch or dinner. When they were a mile from the target area pinpointed by Indianapolis, they stopped and gathered for a final briefing.

Laurie and Pete were now in charge and their FBI training was oblivious . No more jokes, no more kidding around. It was now serious business.

Pete said, "We will continue one more mile and we'll be on

the southern edge of the search area. At that point we will space the vehicles about fifty yards apart and drive slowly north. Upon any sightings or indications of humans, the spotting vehicle will radio the other vehicles reporting what has been sighted. Everyonewill have their radio receivers on standby."

Jason asked, "So, when do we go after them?"

"Nobody is to proceed until I have given the signal by radio. If we see anyone and they try to run, do not panic. We will catch up with them. We have the finest trackers in the world. If there is gunfire, protect yourself as best as possible. Do not try to be a hero. The prime object is our safety and the safety of Mr. Andrews. Everyone understand that?"

There was no doubt in anyone's' mind who was in charge. They all said yes or nodded their heads.

They proceeded slowly for the next mile. Pete motioned for the vehicles to spread out and wait for his command. The four landrovers moved into position. Pete, his tracker, and driver were in the middle vehicle. Jason, a tracker, and driver was another forty yards on the right. Laurie, with his tracker and driver, was forty yards to Pete's' left. Another two trackers and a driver were fifty yards past Laurie's vehicle.

Pete gave the signal to move forward slowly. Jason held his hand on his new gun holster and took a very deep breath. Their eyes scanned every small detail in the bush. For everything that Jason, Pete, and Laurie saw, the trackers saw ten times more.

They were like human hawks, sharply swinging their heads from left to right

and simultaneously moving their eyes in one flowing motion. Living in South Africa, Laurie knew that these trained men could see an insect moving on a stick many yards away. They could sight a snake lying on a tree branch a hundred feet above their heads. They could spot movement far beyond what Jason, Pete or any tourist could see.

They slowly rode through the bush, off the road, over the fallen limbs, softly bouncing and swaying back and forth. They tried to be as quiet as they could.

One thing that went through Jason's mind was that nobody could live out here unless they knew what they were doing. They would have to hire a tracker just like he did. It might be harder than he thought to find Andrews, but at least with the microchips, they could continue to track him.

As they passed the one-mile mark, Jason knew something was wrong. The microchip should have been more accurate than that. He called Jim Kraft on the open, wireless line.

"Jim, where the hell is he, we've gone about a mile and there's no sign of anything!" Jason whispered into his cell phone.

"Jason, he's right there, he's right on top of you, or you're right on top of him!"

"Bullshit, Jim, he's not here. We've got four land rovers spread out covering 200 yards, and believe me, the trackers we have with us could spot anything that moves!"

"Well, maybe Mr. Andrews isn't moving. Maybe he's completely still because you have now passed him! We're showing your chip now moving away from his."

"Oh, Jesus Christ, Jim, adjust your damn computer!"

"I'm telling you, Jason, you're moving past him!"

Jason grabbed the microphone in his vehicle and called Pete.

"Pete, Pete, can you hear me," Jason said in a muffled voice.

"Yes, Jason, what is it?"

"Indianapolis says we've gone past Andrews' chip. At one time we were right on it."

"What? You've got to be frigging kidding me!" Pete whispered.

Pete immediately changed the mobile phone frequency and stopped all the land rovers and added, "Ok, fellows, let's get together for a little discussion."

All the vehicles gathered around Pete's land rover.

Pete spoke softly, "Ok guys, Jason is on the phone with Indianapolis and their computer says we overshot our target. Let's turn the rovers around and try it one more time. This time, keep your eyes peeled because there is a human being there somewhere. We just missed him."

All the vehicles turned the opposite direction and spaced out.

On Pete's signal, they all started again slowly. The trackers were a little embarrassed, because they are not used to missing something that big and important. They thought they were the best, and they were.

The sweep was even more deliberate this time. The group looked up, down and around. Several minutes later they were back where they started, and had seen nothing. Pete was pissed. Jason was not very polite to Jim Kraft on the cell phone. The facial expressions of the rest of the group revealed their disappointment, not to mention that it seemed to be a giant a waste of time for them.

Jason cupped his hand around his the cell phone, trying to be quiet, and said, "Ok, Jim, where the hell are we and where the hell is Andrews?"

Jim answered, "You went past him the first time and now came back past him again. We're sitting here watching the whole damn thing."

"You're out of your friggin mind," Jason replied. "We're looking at trees and bushes and there's almost nowhere for anyone to hide. It's pretty sparse out here and Andrews ain't invisible."

"Well, wait a minute, Jason," Jim said. "Is it possible that they could have him buried in a ground bunker or a fake mound? Nothing else makes much sense from what you say."

"You've been reading too damn many Alex Cross mysteries. How in the hell could someone exist out here in an underground bunker or mound?" Jason snapped back.

"Hell Jason, I don't know. You're the great white hunter running around South Africa. I'm setting here in Indianapolis!"

Jason looked at Pete and Laurie and slowly said, "Ok, can we make one more pass and look for underground bunkers?"

Pete said, "Sure, why not, and while we're there, we'll look for see-thru houses and invisible tents, how about a Harry Potter invisible cloak!" Laurie laughed and Jason frowned again.

The group turned around, assumed their positions. This time Pete had the trackers get out of the vehicles and walk on foot looking for human tracks. They started slowly back through the area. As they proceeded even slower, the trackers kept looking on the ground for any type of evidence that someone had been in the area. If they could look at an old lion paw print and tell how long ago the print was made, they should be able to, at least, locate a human footprint.

The trackers stomped on any suspected ground, scraped the ground with their feet and kept shaking their heads in a motion that could be interpreted as, "This is really stupid!"

Pete also thought it was stupid and after covering a mile and said,

"Ok, that's it for the day, let's go back to the camp and have a drink!"

No one argued. The group turned back around, drove through the area again. This time their enthusiasm waned, and getting back to camp became the focal point. Jason called Indianapolis and was not happy about the performance of Pinpoint, Inc. He also had a long talk with Higgie about the chip that couldn't be found. She offered no advice, but insisted the chip worked.

Jim Kraft said he had been working on the computer program all afternoon and could find nothing wrong. It had correctly followed Jason's chip and there was no reason it would not track Mr. Andrews. There was a slight chance that Andrews' chip had malfunctioned; however, it was still giving information on his body temperature.

Jim said to Jason, "I will stay here all night and continue to work on the problem. Will you go back into the bush tomorrow?"

"You're damn right we'll go back tomorrow," Jason blurted out. "I'm not leaving here without Harold Andrews!"

"What if the chip is not in him?" Jim said. "What if it's just laying out on the ground or hidden somewhere?"

We're going back out there tomorrow and that's that! If we find nothing, we'll decide what the next step should be.

Jim answered, "Ok, Great White Hunter, I've grown fond of you and your perseverance. We'll give it one more shot tomorrow morning."

After the phone call, Pete wished Jason good luck.

Jason paused and said, "Thanks, this is real important to the image of the company and I've got to make this work."

"I know, and I want it to work, too." Pete replied.

They toasted and enjoyed the sounds and the scenery.

The dinner in the Boma was great. They feasted on, of all things, grilled Impala and other tasty items like buffalo, giraffe and crocodile. After sitting around an open bonfire and exchanging stories, they were ready to turn in. Addie told them,

"Remember to check under your bed covers before getting into bed. Sometimes crawly things like to slip under the bed covers and you don't want to be in bed with a Black Mamba. If a Black Mamba snake bites you, chances are you will not have time to go anywhere for anti-serum. Their poison takes only minutes before you can kiss your ass goodbye. Most rangers and trackers carry the anti-serum with them. So, when you get in your room, in Africa, you look everywhere before you do anything. And, in the morning, be sure to check inside your shoes. They are nice and warm and a wonderful place for things to crawl inside."

Needless to say, Pete and Jason were not amused with the warning.

The next morning they were up at five for a light breakfast. At 6:30 they were back in the land rovers ready for the trek back to the search area. Jason had called Indy and was told that Andrews had only moved slightly during the night, but he did move. This time they needed some results, or Jason and his company might be in big trouble.

They retraced the entire search area three times with no results. Pete told Jason they were returning to the camp and retuning to Johannesburg. They would have a conference call with their headquarters and leave for New York the next day.

CHAPTER ELEVEN

SAVE THE COMPANY

The evening before Pete was to return to New York, and Laurie was to go back to Johannesburg, Jason met them for dinner in the lodge.

Pete spoke with concern, "Jason, I'm really sorry this didn't work out.

I know you have put a lot of work into your company, I hope you can figure out what went wrong and get back on track."

"I don't think anything is wrong, I just think we're missing something here. The company will survive. I know we have a good product."

Pete sighed, "Jason, we've been over that area six times and there's nothing out there. I wish we could find something, but, there's nothing there but underbrush and dangerous creatures."

"I can't answer that, Pete, but I know our system works and Harold Andrews has got to be somewhere in Kruger Park."

Pete replied, "Well, the chip isn't walking around by itself. Do you think Andrews and his chip is buried somewhere, and if so, who in the hell could have done it?"

"The chip is capable of providing information about body heat. We would know if Harold Andrews is dead and buried somewhere in the bush. But, since the chip is still showing body temperature, he's got to be still alive and he's got to be here somewhere."

"You keep assuming that the chip is still in Mr. Andrews but you don't know that," Laurie chimed in.

Jason snapped back, "Ok, let's say it's not in Andrews, it's in someone else. But even if it is, hells fire, we should be able to see somebody!"

"Exactly!" Laurie said. "That's why there has to be something wrong either with your system or the microchip. Maybe the satellite directional signal is off and he's somewhere in south Jersey!"

"I don't know, Laurie, but I'm staying because I've got to figure out what the problem is. My entire company is on the line."

Pete interrupted," Well, I wish we could stay and help, but we've got an investigation to conduct. We have to find Andrews with or without your company. I talked to my boss this evening and he wants us back in upper New York where they found the car. We are going to start all over again from the beginning. I'm sorry." There was an honest sadness in his voice. Pete had become not only a business associate of Jason, but also a friend.

"What about your partner, Jane, who's in Indianapolis?" Jason said.

"I've talked to Jane. She will be flying to New York tomorrow to meet me. I have convinced my boss to have the agency stay in direct contact with your company. I believe in you, and I'm sure you will be able to give us guidance as soon as you smooth out the bumps in your system."

Jason said, "I'm calling Higgie tonight and bringing her down here to help. If there are bumps in the chip, she will figure it out. If it's in the satellite system, Jim will figure that out."

Laurie said, "Jason, if you need to go back to meet your assistant at the airport, Addie can get you on the plane with us tomorrow morning and I will help with your arrangements in Jo-burg."

The three men made small talk for a short time, drank some coffee, agreed to meet for breakfast, and retired to their rooms.

Jason was tired of hearing about the bumps in his company's systems. He was still convinced that there was another answer to the mystery of Mr. Andrews' location. He called Higgie in Indianapolis.

"Hi Higgie, you have to come and help me. I don't understand what's going on here. Jim says Andrews is here, but we can't find anything. I know the system works and it's really important that we find him or the company's in trouble.

"Jason, what will I be able to do there that I can't do here?"

"Well Higgie, a little moral support would be worth a lot at this time. I need to exchange ideas and talk to someone." He said this with a tone of helplessness in his voice.

"Ok, Jason, I'll be in Johannesburg as soon as I can. Will you meet me at the airport?"

"Of course, I'll meet you there. I'll fly back to Johannesburg tomorrow and get rooms at the Santon Sun Intercontinental. You let me know when you will arrive and I'll be there with bells on." His voice was already more cheerful and relaxed.

"Ok, Jason, I'll call you at Londolozi later today. Take care of yourself, I'm worried about you."

"Really? That really makes my day. I kinda miss having you round."

She paused just to take in that comment. "Ok, I'll see you either tomorrow night or the night after. I'll call you either way."

They said good night, and hung up.

Jason called Addie and Laurie and asked for help in making arrangements to meet Higgie in Jo-berg.

Addie made the arrangements for Jason to return to Jo-Berg with Pete and Laurie. They would leave tomorrow at mid-morning. She also made arrangements for Jason and Higgie to return in two days and stay at Londolozi at a discount rate even though the FBI had departed. Jason also asked her to arrange for two drivers and two trackers when they returned.

Laurie made reservations for Jason at the Santon Sun hotel and offered a car and driver to use while in Jo-berg. He also arranged dinner at the same restaurant that he had taken Pete and Jason on their first night.

When Higgie called Jason with her arrangements she told him that Jim was doing a complete check of their entire system.

"Jason, I've gone over and over the computerized performance of the microchip in Andrews and there isn't any reason to think it's not working correctly. Jim and I both agree that the body temperature readings are a little off, but we can't figure out if that could be a function of the mechanics of the chip or if Andrews has a medical problem. We don't think it's a mechanical problem."

She continued, "We have received a call from Samuel Rome in New York and he wants to talk to you as soon as possible. He will not talk to anyone else. He sounded really upset and we told him we would contact you and have you call him as soon as possible."

"Thanks Higgie, I have his number, I'll call him right away. I will see you tomorrow afternoon. I'll be there with bells on."

"I can't wait to see that," She said, with a giggle in her voice.

They said goodbye.

Jason took a deep breath and called Samuel in New York.

PINPOINT INC.

The phone rang in Rome's office. The secretary passed him through to Mr. Rome. "Hello, this is Samuel Rome."

"Mr. Rome, this is Jason Higgins."

"Mr. Higgins, I understand you are in South Africa."

"Yes sir, I'm in a game reserve several miles north of Johannesburg. I hope you are well. Its 8:30 p.m. here. Is it 1:30 p.m. in New York?"

"Yes, it's 1:30 here. Have you made any progress finding Mr. Andrews?"

"No, sir, we haven't located Mr. Andrews, but we're continuing to search this area. Our systems in Indianapolis tell us that he is still here and alive. We intend to find him."

"Are you sure he has been in South Africa ever since he disappeared? Are you sure he has been there ever since the first day I called you?"

"Yes sir, we are. He was probably here before then. We don't know how long he's been missing."

"Jason, we had a considerable amount of money embezzled from our company five days ago. We just discovered it today. As soon as we discovered that Mr. Andrews disappeared, we decided to audit our funds to make sure that whoever had Mr. Andrews couldn't use him to get access to our systems. That was four days ago. I guess we were a little late. We notified you seven days ago that he was missing and you told us that he was in South Africa. That means he wasn't even in the country when the embezzlement happened!"

"How do you know when this happened?" Jason asked.

"Our security and reporting systems record all transactions. I told you that transactions were done by handprint identification. Our systems will not transfer cash without this security procedure. The transactions were made five days ago, obviously with an authorized handprint. However, it could have not been Mr. Andrews' handprint if he was in South Africa."

Jason asked, "You mean, Mr. Andrews had to be in your offices five days ago when the transaction happened?"

"Well, I suppose a copy of the handprint, or just the hand, without a body, might have fooled our system. I'd like to tell you that everything we do here is perfect, but we've discovered shortcomings in our systems. Sometimes we need to delay sending transactions because our client must transfer other funds in order to cover the transaction. Therefore, we can set our computer transfer system to delay a transfer. The number of days we can delay the transfer is unlimited. Our reporting systems will record when the transfer actually occurs, but not the date the transaction was programmed in advance."

"So, you don't know when the transaction was set up, only when the system actually transferred the funds," Jason asked

"That's correct," Samuel answered.

"Do you know if Mr. Andrews was the person who transferred the funds?" Jason asked.

"The records did have his name on the transaction, but we cannot verify that his handprint actually made the transaction. There are many other people in the company who can transfer ten million dollars with their handprint."

"Wow," Jason replied. "Ten million dollars is missing?"

"No, Jason, 100 million dollars is missing. There were ten transactions of ten million dollars each."

"Holy mother of God!" Jason gasped. "Surly, you can trace it."

"Well, that's another flaw we discovered in our system. The money was transferred from five separate accounts to banks that are commonly used for those accounts. Each of these clients has several banks and account numbers set up to transfer funds. It was very difficult to catch, but our audits discovered that all ten of these transfers were sent to the clients' banks. However, they were sent to new account numbers that we do not recognize."

Jason asked, "So, is the money in those accounts?"

"No, Jason, unfortunately it's not that easy. As soon as the withdrawal time limitations were up, the money in each account was transferred to unknown accounts in Zurich Switzerland. That was four days ago.

"You mean the money can't be traced?" Jason said with amazement.

"As far as I know now, the answer is no. We have federal authorities and international banking officials working on that right now. However, you know about banking accounts in Switzerland. They really protect their clients with total privacy."

"Which of your clients lost money?"

"Five OPEC countries. I'd rather not say which ones right now. We have notified them and they are obviously not pleased with us."

"Are you insured?" Jason asked slowly.

"That's a real good question. Yes, we have insurance. We don't know if we are covered in this situation. There are certain types of losses that are not covered. We're not sure how this situation will be viewed by our insurance company."

"Well, Mr. Rome, we will do everything we can to help you solve this problem. Miss Higginbothem is flying to South Africa tomorrow to help in our search. The FBI has decided to focus their investigation where Mr. Andrews' car was discovered. We can tell you at this time that he is still alive because the chip is functioning properly."

Jason continued in a quizzical voice, "Mr. Rome, I'm just

curious about something. Is their any way someone could make a mold of Mr. Andrews hand out of silicone, or something like that, which could fool your security system?"

"Christ, Jason, I don't know if that's possible. I would think that our system could detect something like that, but we've never had to find out."

"Until now," Jason said in a soft voice.

"Yes, Jason, until now."

Jason said, "I will get back in touch with you as soon as I can. Meanwhile, please keep Jim Kraft, at our offices in Indianapolis informed with any information you can share with us. We will solve this problem, Mr. Rome."

"Thank you, Jason, I know you will do the best you can."

Jason pushed the "off" button on his cell phone, fell into deep thought for a moment, then went back to the lodge bar for a stiff vodka martini, maybe two, maybe more.

When he returned to his cottage and was in bed, Jason could hear the nightly sounds outside and knew they might keep him awake. Although he had a thick, stonewall between him and whatever was out there, he felt uncomfortable. For a brief moment he thought about tomorrow, when they found his shredded body and everyone said, "How in the hell did that thing get in his room? He seemed like such a nice guy!"

Even with the outside African sounds, he finally fell to sleep.

Jason was awake before the alarm went off the next morning. He packed, had some coffee in his room and went to the lodge to meet Pete and Laurie. Addie was having breakfast with the lodges' general manager on the veranda overlooking the bush and under a large tree that covered the entire veranda. He stopped to talk to her.

"Hello Addie, hope all is well with you."

"Oh, Hi, Mr. Higgins, all your arrangements have been made?"

"Thank you, you're a big help."

"I got you two suites. I put them both in your name. They will be next to each other."

"That's fine." Jason replied.

Just then Jason saw Pete and Laurie come into the room. He thanked Addie again and joined the pair at their table on the veranda.

Jason said cheerfully, "Good morning, gentlemen. Did you sleep well?"

Pete gave Jason a frowned look and replied, "Oh sure, like I was lying in a totally dark bedroom, on a stormy night, in a horror movie!"

Jason grinned. "That bad, huh?" he said.

"I've never heard so many damn scary sounds in one place in my life. It sounds like every animal is just outside waiting for you to come out."

Laurie said, "Pete, you've got a stone wall between you and the outside. There's nothing on the outside that can get in, only things that are already in the inside!"

"Oh, that really helps. I don't care, it's still creepy!" Pete replied.

Jason held his hand over his heart and said, "Oh, that makes us all feel so good, our big, bad FBI guy is afraid of the dark!"

They all laughed, except Pete.

All of a sudden Jason jumped right out of his chair screaming: "God Damn it!" Pete and Laurie both jerked back from the table and jumped out of their chairs.

"What? What?" Pete yelled.

Sitting next to the bowl of apples on the tabletop was a tan, skinny monkey staring back at the three men. He had jumped from the tree limb on to the table, to steal an apple. It was something that he probably did every morning. A waiter came running out of the kitchen yelling, "Out! Out! Get away! Get away!" The monkey looked casually at the waiter, and then at Jason, and jumped back up into the tree. The waiter said, "Sorry," and went back into the kitchen. The monkey continued to jump around the lower tree branches waiting for another chance to get back on the table, but Jason, Pete and Laurie made growling noises and waving jesters to keep him away.

Soon the waiter came back with a hand-made sling shot. He put a small rock into the cradle and shot the rock at the monkey. The monkey ignored the rock that flew by his head, a response that indicated that the waiter had probably never actually hit a monkey. So, there was no alarm.

After breakfast, Jason, Jake and Laurie were sipping coffee and protecting the apples from the monkey when a couple of local guides came onto the veranda. They spoke to Pete.

"We're ready to go when you are, sir. We have your luggage in the Land Rover."

Pete and Jason thanked the guides and the general manager and walked to the parking area.

The ride back to Skukuza airport was another game ride.

They saw more impala, giraffe, monkeys and elephants. The ride wasn't any smoother than before.

When they reached the airport their twin-engine plane was parked on the narrow asphalt runway. Several passengers were ready to load. This flight was a regular scheduled flight and not chartered.

Upon arrival at the Johannesburg airport Jason thanked Pete and asked him to keep in close touch. Pete, in turn, made Jason promise to be careful in the bush.

"Thanks, Pete, I'll be careful."

Pete laughed. "And don't shoot yourself in the ass either!" he chidingly commented. Then he paused and said, "Never mind, I'm not sure you could hit it!"

They both laughed and shook hands, as friends do. Then Jason turned to Laurie, "Thanks for all your help. I appreciate the time you spent with us."

"You're welcome, and if you need any help, just call me."

"I will," Jason replied. Then they all went their separate ways.

It would be almost a day before Higgie would arrive. So Jason took the car and driver that Laurie had arranged and went to the Santon Sun Hotel.

At the hotel, Jason received a call from Higgie.

"Jason, I'm in Atlanta. I'll be leaving soon. We arrived two hours late and I'm getting on the underground tram to go to the departure gate. I'm not sure I'm going to make the flight, but I'll try. If I don't make it, I'll call you back. If I do, and you don't hear from me in the next hour, you'll know I'm on my way. Everything ok down there?"

"It will be a lot better when you're here. Pete is on his way back to New York and we're pretty much on our own. I think I've made all the arrangements we'll need. So get yourself down here."

"I'm on my way."

Higgie's plane landed one hour late. Jason was there to meet her in the baggage area. He spotted her coming out of the luggage area and yelled, "Over here! I was starting to worry you might have missed the flight."

Higgie yelled out over a few people, "Hey, you're dealing

with a world traveler here." She walked towards Jason with her arms outstretched, obviously looking for a hug.

The hug was businesslike, but never the less, a hug.

She added, "What? Miss my flight and an opportunity to go to South Africa and be with a man who needs a woman to help him survive? I wouldn't miss that!"

"Ok, Superwoman, let's go. I have a car and driver just outside the door."

On the way to the hotel he told Higgie all that had happened over the last four days. He showed signs of concern about the chip and the tracking system, something he had not done before.

"My God, Higgie, if we don't figure this out, we're going to be in trouble with other clients. The word will get out sooner or later."

Higgie moved a little closer in the back seat and said; "Don't worry, we'll figure it out."

They checked in the hotel, confirmed tomorrow's flight to Skukuza airport and walked to dinner in the shopping mall.

They sat in the corner of the restaurant next to the window that showed a beautiful African moon. If they had been lovers, it would have been perfect, but being business associates, they could only let those feelings wander around in their heads.... and they did wander.

The food was wonderful. The South African wine came from the cool slopes of the Constantiaberg valley and from the country's oldest cellars at Groot Constantia. All in all, the dinner and atmosphere were perfect, although somewhat wasted on a handsome young couple who were only business associates.

After dinner they walked through the shops in the mall and made some small purchases to take back to the office for their workmates. When they returned to the hotel they made plans for breakfast. Higgie thanked Jason for dinner and they went to their separate rooms.

Early the next morning they each called for the bellman to check their luggage at the front desk and met for breakfast.

"How did you sleep?" Jason asked.

"Are you kidding me, I was up all night. My body thinks we're still in Inidana. I hope an afternoon nap is in my future."

"Yea, I know. I'm just beginning to sleep through the night and I've been here for several days. I'm sure we can arrange a nap."

"You mean I have to wait for several days to sleep?".

"Well, unless you get drunk and pass out," Jason chirped. They finished breakfast and departed for the airport. At the airport they checked in, went through security and boarded the twin-engine plane. It was another regularly scheduled flight to Skukuza.

When they landed at Skukuza Jason saw the Londolozi Land Rover and the two guides. They departed and Jason introduced Higgie to the two guides. They immediately drove the bouncy, dirt road to Londolozi. Along the way Jason and the guides pointed out several hyena, a small herd of buffalo, two giraffe, four elephants and, of course, many impalas who would be on the wildlife menu again today.

When they reached Londolozi, Addie met them and announced that she had pre-checked them in and arranged lunch on the varanda.

They went to the veranda and while waiting on lunch, and fighting off the monkey that stole apples, Jason called Jim Kraft at his home back in Indianapolis.

Jim answered his phone from a sound sleep. After Jason apologized for the early call he asked Jim if he could get to the office early because he and Higgie were going into the bush and needed his guidance.

Jim replied, "Of course I will. I planned to be there by 6:00 a,m. today. I knew you would be calling in this morning. When you get ready, just call."

Jason confirmed that he would stay on an open line with Indianapolis starting at 3:00 p.m. South African time, which would be 7:00 a.m. in Indiana.

After lunch Jason and Higgie went to their suites and unpacked. They met again at 2:00 p.m. on the veranda. The monkey was still there looking for food. The waiter with the slingshot was collecting small rocks.

At 3:00 p.m. Jason called Jim on his cell phone to say they were ready.

"I'm ready," Jim replied. "You need to go back to the same location you were three days ago. Andrews is back in that area."

"Gotcha Jim, we're on our way."

Jason, Higgie, a driver, and a tracker were in one land rover and a driver and tracker were in another. They drove the same route and arrived at the area where they started their search a few days ago. Their driver commented on the number of other vehicles in the area.

"We have quite a group of vehicles in this area today. We have seen a lot of rovers and large vans all over the park recently. They belong to the park rangers. They thin out the various herds and groups of animals now and then. They have been working around here for over a month. If there are too many animals trying to feed in the same area, it's not good for the ecology of the entire park, so they take some out. They either kill them or sometime sell them."

The two rovers separated about fifty yards apart, just enough to be able to see each other now and then. They began their slow drive through the area where Jim Kraft said the microchip was now located.

After they passed over the area four times, Jason told the guide to take them back to Londolozi. Kraft had told Jason that their two chips were shown to be together a couple times. This was really upseting and disappointed Jason. He was also really bewildered and a little pissed.

Back at the lodge Jason made arrangements to go back to the area early the next morning. He and Higgie agreed to meet for dinner in the lodge at 7:30.

At 7:20 Jason was at the bar in the lodge when Higgie walked in. When he saw her he thought to himself, what a wonderful, beautiful gal she was. He also gave some serious thought to the knockout body she had.

Higgie joined Jason at the bar and ordered a Grey Goose Martini with double olives. That's exactly what Jason was already drinking.

The setting for dinner was even more romantic than the dinner last evening in Johannesburg. There was something about being out in the middle of the bush, with only a few other people at the lodge, that gave a sense of being very alone and un-noticed.

After a wonderful dinner of wild game and vegetables they had another Grey Goose Martini, with double olives, in the lounge. It was time to call it a night. They walked out of the lodge, along the winding rock path to their suites that were actually small bungalows about thirty yards from the lodge. As they walked they leaned closer to each other, as if a wild animal might just be hiding just off the path. In fact, that might be true. They had been told to be careful walking anywhere outside the lodge, especially at night. The lodge always had workers outside watching for unwanted animals.

The farther they walked the slower they walked, both commenting on what a lovely night it was and what a shame it was to be ending. When they reached the door to her bungalow, she paused to find her room key. Actually, it was attached to a very large wooden cheetah and easy to locate, but she fumbled around in her purse anyway.

She put the key in the lock, opened the door, but did not make a move to go in. She turned to Jason, stood close and said, "Oh, Jason, it was a perfect night."

"Yea, it was, wasn't it?" He said as he looked into those beautiful light blue eyes.

There was a long pause when neither spoke, they just stood there and looked in each other. It was awkward, but romantic.

"I'm sorry I hired you," Jason said softly.

"I'm sorry I took the job," She said even softer.

There was another pause until it was obvious that each were holding their breath and tilting their head in different directions. They moved a little closer to each other when Jason said, "We are co-workers and"……He didn't finish the sentence when she said, "I quit," and moved her lips on his. It was a soft exploring kiss with controlled passion. When he put his arms around her waist he could feel the small little grove that was just above the upper curve of her butt. His middle fingers moved into that wonderful crevasse and their kiss became much more explosive.

She leaned up off her toes to position her hips closer to his, although she was too short to actually get where she wanted to be. He squeezed his strong forearms together and lifted her into the position she was hoping for. The kiss went on for a long time. Maybe it was two kisses, maybe three.

When they finally pulled their lips apart, their bodies stayed close together, neither wanting to end this incredible moment.

Jason said softly, even though he was breathing hard, "You can't quit. You're fired."

"Well, if I don't work for you any more, why don't you come in and see where I live....please?"

"I'd be delighted, but I don't think we have a chaperone," he said in a playful tone.

"I don't think we need one," she said in a low, sexy voice. He half picked her up, half dragged her into the bungalow. They did not part their bodies during the entire movement from the front door to the large oversized African bed. Once in the room, with the sounds of the bush outside, they melted their bodies together and found another world, another time, a new life.

The sun didn't wake them up. They didn't need the sun. The closeness of each other only allowed them to catch short naps and not long sleep periods. They did not waste their time together by just sleeping.

At 8:00 a.m. the phone rang. It was the Londolozi operator with Higgie's wake up call.

"Oh damn, I forgot I left a wake up call," she said as she slammed the phone down. "We could just act like we didn't get it?"

Jason groaned, "As good as that sounds, we have some work ahead of us. However, hold that thought for a later time."

'Oh, I see. I'm back on the payroll again!" She said with a professional, flirting voice. "What if I quit, again?"

"Well, then you'll loose all your benefits!"

"What benefits?" she said sortly.

"All your new benefits that we just added to your compensation package last night!"

"Ok, Ok, I'm up!" she said laughingly.

Jason, after a few more tender moments, went back to his room to freshen up. They agreed to meet in thirty minutes.

In thirty minutes they were on the veranda. The monkey was waiting to steal some food from their breakfast plates. The waiter had his weapon.

An hour later they were still on the veranda. Jason had made arrangements to go back into the bush just after noon. Although that would be early morning in Indiana, Jim Kraft would have the time to get to the office and organize for the hunt.

There would be nothing Jason and Higgie could do until after noon, unless of course, it might be what was rushing through both their minds since 8:15 this morning. However, there would still be time for romance later if each could figure out a way for the other to have the idea first.

At 11:30 they were back on the veranda having lunch with the monkey.

Addie came to their table with a note in her hand.

"This came in for you just a while ago. It sounds urgent."

The note said, "Call me immediately, and I mean now." Jim Kraft. Jason went back to his room and punched in Jim's number on his cell phone.

"Hello, Jim Kraft."

"Jim, It's Jason."

"Holy Shit, Jason, where the hell have you been?"

"I've been right here. I left my cell phone in my room. Why? What's wrong?"

"You won't friggin' believe this, but Mr. Andrews in on his way back towards Johannesburg!"

"What? What the hell do you mean? How in the hell do you know that?" Jason shouted.

"Hey, remember me, I'm the guy with the satellite system. When I got to the office a while ago, Andrews was not in the old

location. At this very moment he has moved fro
the local airport at Kruger Park. He's stationary
like he might be on a plane soon, probably to Jonann.

"Ok, Jim, we are on our way. We'll get to Johannesbu.
as quickly as we can. I'll call you back. Stay in touch with him, wherever he goes!"

"OK, Jason."

Jason asked Addie how fast they could get to Johannesburg. She said that the last scheduled flight for the day was leaving in ten minutes. A charter might be possible, if one was in the area. She would check.

Jason and Higgie went to their suites and packed. Addie called Jason's suite about twenty minutes later.

"Mr. Higgins, I'm sorry, there are no charter flights available this afternoon.

You will have to wait until tomorrow morning and take the morning scheduled flight that you and the other two gentlemen took a couple days ago. I have booked you and Miss Higginbothem on that flight."

"We have no other options?" Jason asked

"No sir, I'm sorry."

The bad news was that they would have to wait almost eighteen hours to leave for Johannesburg. The good news was that it gave him another night with Higgie in the cottage suite……... if, he could get her to agree to another wonderful night together, which shouldn't be too tough.

Jason waited an hour or so and called Jim Kraft. Jim reported that Andrews had indeed boarded the plane and was approaching Johannesburg.

An hour later Jim called to say that Andrews was in the Johannesburg airport, or actually stationary just outside the airport. He told Jason he would call if there was any movement.

That night they had dinner in the Boma. Higgie loved it. The food was good, the drinks were stiff, the night was clear and the moon was bright. Surly chances were high for another night of romance if Jason could make it happen without looking like a sexual predator.

Jason and Higgie strolled back to their cottages in the cool moonlight. It was another stop at Higgie's door, another warm passionate kiss and another crash and drag through the doorway. The night was beautiful and events in Higgie's cottage were even more beautiful. They had found each other's companionship and hearts. It was complicated, but it was good.

Thoughts of Cindy Hassel never once came into Jason's mind.

The phone rang at 7:00 a.m. next to Higgie's bed. The two people in the bed were wide awake and had been for some time. She picked it up quickly, thanked the operator, and slammed it back down again.

"It was a wrong number," She said.

"Been getting a lot of those lately?" he asked.

"I guess we'll have to unplug the phone."

"Or have it removed."

They giggled and put a strangle hold on each other. About thirty minutes later they finally agreed to get out of bed. It wasn't easy.

He went back to his cottage, took a shower, and packed.

They left their luggage in front of their doors to be picked up by the driver, and went to the veranda to see if the monkey had left any food for breakfast.

Just as they were finishing breakfast their driver came to their table to say he was ready to leave for the Skukuza airport.

They thanked Addie and the other staff and went to the parking lot.

While they drove to Skukuza, the guide pointed out various interesting sights in the bush. They saw many more animals, including a pride of lions walking slowly through the bush. The lead lion was an old male who had many scars on his face from protecting his position with his females. There were three females and two cubs in his pride.

When they arrived at the airport they were full of dust and ready to get on the plane. They only had to wait about forty minutes to board and depart. Still no word from Jim Kraft.

When the plane arrived in Johannesburg, they met their car and driver that was on loan from Laurie. Jason called Jim Kraft immediately on his cell phone.

"Jim Kraft, can I help you?"

"Jim, It's Jason. What do you have?"

"He's still in the airport!" Jim said quickly.

Jason shouted, "Where in the airport?"

"Hell, I don't know, but he's there somewhere," Jim retorted,

"OK. OK. We'll start looking around. I'll call you back or you call me if he leaves!" Jason exclaimed.

Jason hung up and looked at Higgie." Let's go, he's here in the airport!" he said.

They went to the front of the airport.

"Let's hang here for a minute. Maybe he's planning on leaving the airport," Jason said.

"That doesn't make any sense," replied Higgie. "He would have left the airport a long time ago if he wasn't getting on a plane."

"Right!" Jason said. "Let's check the airline check-ins to the States!"

They went to the airline counters that had flights to the USA and asked if a Harlold Andrews was on any of those flights. As a cover they told the counter agents that he was their uncle and they were trying to contact him.

They could not find him booked on any flight. They searched the airport for another two hours when Jason's cell phone rang.

"Hello, Hello," Jason said.

"Jason, It's Jim. He's moving! He's moving away from the airport!"

"Can you tell which direction?' Jason exclaimed.

"Yes, he's moving east, away from the airport!" Jim said.

Jason spun around and got his bearings. "Hell, that's out the back of the airport where the runways are. He must be on a plane getting ready to leave. I'll go see what flights are leaving now and I'll call you back." Jason pushed the cell phone "off" button and they rushed to the large panel listing airline departures. They looked up and down the large panel. Jason said, "Look for all the flights that are scheduled within the next five to ten minutes." They scanned the panel and Higgie said, "There's a flight to Cape Town and one to Madagascar."

Jason said, "There's one to Madrid, one to Paris, and one to Lisbon."

Higgie added, "And one to Singapore."

"Shit!" Jason said. "He could be on any of them or, they could be on one of them. He's probably not by himself!"

Ten minutes later Jason's phone rang.

"Hello!"

"Jason, It's Jim. He's on an airplane and moving fast. Going south!"

"South? Jason yelled. "There ain't nothing south of here

except the Pole! That's not the way to the States or Europe!" Jason groaned.

"Ok, Jason, you and Higgie hang loose. I'll call you as soon as we know where he might be going."

Jason and Higgie found themselves walking around all the shops and waiting areas of the airport. They would sit for a while, walk for a while and sit for a while. Jason was getting tired and anxious.

Jason's phone rang.

"Hello!" Jason shouted.

"Hi, we think he's going to Capetown! The plane is on a straight line to Capetown!"

Jason said, "Sure, he is. How stupid can I be? We had to come through Capetown when we first came to Jo-berg. Most of the flights from the States come through Capetown!"

Jim said, "I think if you booked yourselves to the States and left now, you would save a lot of time, because I bet he's coming back to Atlanta.

You might as well be in the air rather than sitting there in the airport. Even if they go somewhere else, you can follow from Atlanta."

"Good idea, Jim. We'll check which flights are the next ones out. We'll call you when we land. Or, you can track my microchip and know exactly where we are."

"Take care, best to Higgie."

Jason checked with South Africa Air, which is the partner for Delta. They had a flight leaving at 5:00 p.m. for Miami. However, it was not a direct flight; the connection was through Paris. "Forget that," Jason thought.

They also had a flight to Atlanta, via Capetown, at 6:15 p.m. that would arrive at 9:30 the next morning. Bingo! That's the flight they would take.

CHAPTER TWELVE

THE CHASE

The next morning the South African flight circled Atlanta and approached the runway. Twenty minutes later Jason and Higgie were at the gate. They called Jim in Indianapolis.

"Jim, we're in Atlanta."

"Yes, I know, I've been watching you."

"What now?" Jason asked.

"It's really strange. Andrews' plane landed in Atlanta several hours ago but he's still at the airport. Maybe he has a long wait for another flight. He's sure not staying in Atlanta or he would have left the airport a long time ago. I can't tell you exactly where to look, but we show him in the general area of the airport."

"Ok, Jim, we'll start looking around. Damn, Atlanta has five different terminals all connected by underground trams. Hell, he could be in any of them. Oh well, we'll start in this one and go to the other four. Atlanta also has a large central area with shops and restaurants they built to host the Olympics, we'll have to check there too. I'll call you later, or you call me."

They hung up.

Jason and Higgie started searching by walking past all the gate areas. Atlanta is a huge airport. They started in Terminal E, which is for international flights, and worked their way back to Terminal A. They saw nobody who even resembled Harold Andrews. Two hours later Jason called Jim again.

"Jim! We've been to all the terminals and found nothing. I assume he is still here or you would have called me."

"Yes, he's still there. God, he's been here for a long, long time."

Jason took a deep breath. "I don't know what to think. I guess we'll just have to wait him out and stay here in the airport."

"Ok," Jim said. "I'll call you back when he moves again."

Jason replied, "Do we have any other choices?"

"I don't know of one," countered Jim.

"Ok, keep in touch," Jason replied.

They went to another restaurant in the airport for lunch. They had Philadelphia cheese steak sandwiches and fries. They both had a couple beers, just to keep their keen edge!

Five more hours went by. That would mean that Andrews had been in the Atlanta airport for most of the day. What the hell is he doing here? Jason thought to himself.

Jason's phone rang again.

"Jason, he's on the move again! He's moved just outside the airport area. I don't know if he's in a vehicle or in a plane that is taxiing out of the terminal."

"OK, stay on the line and tell me as soon as you get a better idea."

The line was silent for several minutes and then Jim came back on line. "It's a plane," he shouted. "He just went from a slow speed to a really fast burst of speed. The plane is circling the airport headed north."

"Keep on him Jim," Jason said.

"I got him, but he's still circling. Now he's moving northwest."

"Let me know when he starts in a straight line," Jason explained.

"He's still turning west and still turning. Now he's going west!" There was a short pause. "Ok, he's straitening up and he's headed pretty much southwest of Atlanta."

"Jim, if he leaves the states, he may be going to Mexico."

"Well, we'll know soon, unless he's headed to the west coast. I'll call you back as soon as I can tell something," Jim said.

They hung up.

Jason told Higgie everything that was going on and she replied, "Ok, let's review. He goes from New York to South Africa for more than a week. Then he flies to Atlanta and spends over twelve hours in the airport. Then he flies west to, wherever! What a mess! I have no idea what's going on."

Thirty minutes later, Jason's phone rang again. It was Jim.

"I think he's turning a little south. He may be going to Mexico."

"Where is he now? Jason said.

"He's just north of the Gulf of Mexico around southern Alabama.

That's kind of on a straight line to Cancun, Mexico." Jason said, "Why in the hell Mexico? Is he headed for the beach?"

Jim exclaimed, "Wait a minute! The plane is turning southeast again. Hold on a minute."

Five minutes later Jim said with a puzzled voice, "It's turning back to the east, somewhere around Mobile, Alabama. Christ! I think it's circling Mobile!"

Four minutes later Jim exclaimed, "It is Mobile! The plane is landing in Mobile!"

"Why the hell Mobile, Alabama?" Jason said, exasperated.

"I don't know, but that's where he is," Jim said.

"Shit, maybe our systems don't work. That doesn't make any sense!" Jason said with an "I give up" tone.

"Look, Jason, the system and the chip works. You need to get your ass down to Mobile," Jim retorted.

"We're not going anywhere until he comes to a stop somewhere. Hell, he may just be changing planes again!" Jason said with a firm voice.

"Call me back when there's no movement."

Jason waited thirty minutes and called Jim back.

"Ok, what's the story now?"

Jim answered, "He's in the Mobile airport and hasn't moved."

Jason said, "Ok, we'll hang around here for a while and you call as soon as you see movement. It's almost 8 o'clock. We're going to get something to eat and check the flights to Mobile."

"Ok, I'll call when something happens," Jim said.

At ten o'clock Jason called Jim from the Atlanta airport.

"Are you still in the office? What's going on?"

"I'm here, but I'd rather be home!" Jim retorted.

"Any movement?" Jason asked.

Jim said, "I would have called you if there had been."

"Well, Higgie and I are tired. So we're going to get a room close to the airport."

"You mean two rooms," Jim said with a chuckle.

"Of course I mean two rooms. Knock it off!" Jason retorted.

Jim said quickly, "Easy, easy, it was just a joke."

"No wise cracks," Jason said with a defensive voice.

They hung up.

Jason and Higgie retrieved their luggage from the holding service, and then went to a big advertisement board that showed all the hotels. They called a hotel next to the airport and booked a room.

Twenty minutes later they were picked up by the hotel van and taken to the hotel. They had one room. Jason thought to himself, should I worry about what Jim knows, or thinks he knows? his answer was, nah!

Jason gave Jim a break and didn't call him until 7:00 a.m. the next day. Jason and Higgie were awake a long time before the telephone call, as they had been for most of the last several mornings.

"Jim, good morning. What's going on?"

Jim sounded like a Mac truck had just run over him. "Nothing new is going on. Andrews is still at the Mobile airport." His voice was shallow and sounded like he had a mouth full of gravel.

"God Jim, you sound terrible."

"Well, I should, I've been here all night."

"Hell, you didn't have to do that." Jason said.

"Yes, I did. If Andrews had moved during the night you would have really been on my ass if someone didn't tell you!"

"Did you get any sleep?" Jason asked.

"Sure, a few hours when I knew planes probably wouldn't be flying," Jim answered.

Jason paused and said, "Why on God's green earth would Andrews stay all night at the airport?"

"I don't know. Why don't you ask him?" Jim said jokingly, trying to lift Jason's sprits.

"I'll do just that when I see him, unless I strangle him first!"

"Are you going to stay there in the hotel until something happens, or are you and Higgie going on to Mobile?"

"I guess so, we can just stay in the room and have room service, or we can get our asses in gear and get to Mobile."

Jim picked up on the Jason's little mistake: "room service to our room."

Jason said quickly, "Well, I mean we each can have room service."

"Sure, you did. I hear nothing. I see nothing. I speak nothing," Jim whispered.

"OK, knock it off. I'll call you again, soon," Jason grunted.

Jason closed the cell phone, turned to Higgie and said, "Hi, where you been all morning?" Room service was cancelled.

Higgie smiled. "Oh, I thought that was room service."

"So, where's the gratuity?" Jason whispered.

Two hours later, when Jason and Higgie arrived at the airport, Jason's phone rang.

"Jason, he's moving again, and I don't think it's by plane!" Jim said in a hurried voice.

"Which way is he going?" Jason said.

"He's going east from the airport. I don't know why, but downtown Mobile is about 14 miles northeast."

"Let me know when he stops. We're getting tickets to Mobile now."

"Ok, I'll call you back. If he's not getting back on a plane it looks like he might be in Mobile for a while. I'll keep a track on him and you call me back."

Jason and Higgie went to the ticket counters and found a flight to Mobile that left in ninety minutes. They bought tickets, had some coffee and donuts and went to the gate.

Their plane landed in Mobile at around noon. They had gained an hour.

When they departed the plane, Jason called Jim.

"We're here. Is he still in the Mobile area?"

"Yes, he's only gone about nine miles east and stopped."

Jason asked," What is nine miles from here?'

Jim replied, "I don't know, but rent a car and I'll guide you to where he is. I've got your chip on the screen."

"Good idea, we're on our way. I'll call you back."

They hung up.

Jason rented a Buick sedan from Hertz and they drove east out of the airport. Jason called Jim.

"Hi, we're out from the airport headed east, What'ya got?"

"You're heading in the right direction. Keep going and I'll let you know when to stop or if you're headed the wrong way."

Jason stayed on the phone line and kept driving east. Jim kept saying; "keep going, keep going, you're right on line."

About 15 minutes later Jim said, "You're getting real close. It should be just ahead of you."

When Jim said, "Stop!" Jason and Higgie looked around. It was a college campus, or some type of campus style school. They drove a couple blocks and saw the sign,"Welcome to the University of South Alabama."

Jim was still on the line and Jason said, "You'll never guess; It's a college campus."

"Which one?" Jim asked.

"South Alabama."

"Well, I'll be damn, I've heard of it, I think they have a good baseball program." Jim said.

"I haven't heard of it, but here we are."

Jim added, "Your chips are real close to each other. You should only be a couple of blocks apart."

"Which way do I go?"

"I can't tell you that. Hell, I've got you real close. You can do something on your own."

"Ok, great! Just because we haven't heard of this place doesn't mean it's a small campus," Jason replied.

"Try going a couple blocks more and I'll see if the chips line up closer."

They drove slowly on down the street.

"Jason, you might turn a little north," Jim said.

Jason made a left hand turn and ran into a dead end street.

"What do you see?" asked Jim.

Jason had a funny urge to say, I see dead people, but instead, said, "I see a bunch of buildings. Hell, it's a college. What the hell would I see?"

"Ok, I got you there. Now it's up to you. I can't get you any closer," Jim replied.

"Jim, do me a favor. Get hold of Pete Donnelly in New York and tell him what's going on. Also, ask him to call me. I have some ideas. Higgie and I are going to have to stay, so would you find the closest Holiday Inn to the campus and book us a room for tonight? Call be back and tell me how to get to the hotel."

"Book you a room? Only one room?"

"No, God damn it, two rooms!" Jason snapped back.

"OK, two rooms….. Just asking," Jim said in a slow, calm voice.

Jason hit his "off" button.

Jason drove the car another block and stopped at the administration building. He had no idea what he was going to say, but they went in anyway. He saw a young lady at the reception desk and asked, "Excuse me, where is the Presidents' office?"

She answered, "It's in this building on the third floor. The elevators are right over there. I don't know if he's in. You'll have to see his secretary."

"Thank You," Jason replied.

They walked to the elevators and went to the third floor.

When the elevator door opened, they looked down a long non-descript hallway. All the doors in the hall looked alike.

They walked to the very end of the hall before they saw Presidents Office on a door.

They opened the door and found a plain, undecorated reception office with an older woman at the desk.

Jason spoke, "Is the President in, Please?"

The lady looked at Jason with a big southern smile and said, "Why sure honey, do you have an appointment?"

"No ma'am I don't, but it's very important that I speak with him. My name is Jason Higgins and I am working on a criminal investigation."

"Oh, my goodness, I hope it doesn't concern someone here at the university."

"I hope not, but that's why I need to talk to the President."

"Just a minute, I'll see if he's available." She disappeared through the door behind her desk.

Three minutes later she reappeared and said, "President Bandy will see you now."

They went around her desk and through the open door.

A gray-haired gentleman in his sixties rose from his desk and introduced himself.

"Welcome to the University. My name is Robert Bandy."

"Good afternoon, President Bandy. My name is Jason Higgins and this is my associate, Paula Higginbothem."

President Bandy asked, "What can I do for you? I understand you are conducting an investigation on our campus. I hope we haven't done anything wrong."

"I don't think so, sir. We are trying to locate a missing person and our information shows he may be located on your campus. Here is his picture." Jason showed a picture of Harold Andrews to President Bandy.

"I'm sorry, I don't recognize him. What can I do to help?"

"Well, we need to know if anyone on your staff flew here from Atlanta yesterday. Or better yet, if anyone just returned from South Africa."

President Bandy said, "Well my staff and many of our employees fly frequently, but I'm sure none have been to South Africa, or I would have known about it. Do you think you're missing person works here?"

"No, we don't, but we have traced our missing person here on a flight from Atlanta this morning. We're trying to figure out why he would come here. Can you find out if any of your people flew from Atlanta this morning?"

President Bandy answered, "If you'll give me some time, I will check with our travel department and see if anyone has been traveling. Give me an hour our so."

"We'll get something to eat and come back in an hour."

The President replied, "We have a nice cafeteria on campus. You might want to eat there and look around."

"We'll do that," Jason said.

President Bandy's secretary gave them directions to the caferteria.

While at the cafeteria, Jason got his call from Pete Donnelly.

"Jason, how the hell are you?"

"Fine, Pete, where are you?"

"I'm in upstate New York. We have retraced Andrews' tracks and have come to a dead end. We are now going over his entire hunting club to see if there are any clues here. Jim Kraft filled me in on everything that has been going on. Wow, what a puzzle."

"Pete, I have an idea, but I need your help."

"Sure, what is it?"

"I would like to check the names on Andrews' flight back from Johannesburg to Atlanta against the names on the flight from Atlanta to Mobile and see if any names match. I can't get that info from the airlines, but you can."

"Sure, I can do that. I'll call you back later."

Jason gave Pete the Andrews flight numbers and departure times that he had looked up just in case they would be useful later.

They hung up.

As they were driving back to President Miller's office, Jason's cell phone rang.

"Jason, it's Pete. We compared the names on the flight from Johannesburg against the names from Atlanta to Mobile and there are no matches. Nobody that came from Johannesburg transferred to the flight to Mobile."

"Oh shit, that's great! I thought we would really have a lead!" He turned to Higgie and said, "No matches!" Higgie took a deep breath and said, "That's too bad. It was a great idea."

"Ok Pete, thanks for the help. We are meeting with the college president in a few minutes. We will let you know if something comes up."

In the President's office, Robert Bandy said, "We did not have anyone fly from Johannesburg to Atlanta, but we did have two laboratory assistants on that flight from Atlanta to Mobile."

Jason, with some excitement in his voice said, "Well, that's something. Who are they?"

"They work in our Primate Research Laboratory."

"That's interesting. What do they do there?" Jason asked.

"They do medical research on squirrel monkies. Primarily they do reproductive biology and behavior studies."

"Do you know what they were doing in Atlanta?" Jason asked.

"Yes, they were meeting a shipment of squirrel monkeys at the Atlanta airport and bringing them back to the university as research animals."

"Jason took a deep breath, heisted, and then asked, "Where did they get the shipment from?"

"South Africa," Robert Bandy answered.

Jason looked quickly at Higgie. Her mouth was open and no words were coming out. Neither could say a word. Their lips were locked. They could not believe what was going through their minds.

"Oh, my god," Jason shouted. "The damn chip is inside one of those monkeys! Hell, no wonder we couldn't fine Harold Andrews, he wasn't even in South Africa! We should have been looking for a damn monkey that for some unbelievable reason has his chip!"

Higgie finally spoke. "How did our chip, I mean Harold Andrews' chip, get in a monkey, a monkey in South Africa? What in the hell is going on?"

"And why?" exclaimed Jason.

President Bandy was really confused by all the comments and said,

"What are you folks talking about? What Chip?"

Jason gave him a quick explanation of Harold Andrews' disappearance and Pinpoint, Inc.'s involvement in the search. He then asked,

"We will need to find the monkey with the chip and remove it. Do we have your permission?"

"Of course," replied President Bandy. "When do you want to do that?"

Jason, excited, said, "As soon as we can. Can we go to the lab now?"

"Of course, I'll make all the arrangements. My secretary will tell you how to get there. It's real close."

Jason and Higgie almost ran out of President Bandy's office. On the way to their car they called Jim Kraft in Indianapolis.

"Jim, you won't God Damn believe what's happened!"

"What; what!" Jim shouted back.

Jason went over the entire story with Jim. It sounded like a fictional story that just couldn't be true. When Jason ended the story with what they found in Mobile, he said, "We're coming back to Indianapolis as soon as we get the chip out of the monkey. We will need to get with Pete Donnelly and show him that our system does work. We were just looking for a human being in Africa and should have been looking up in the trees for a damn monkey! Harold Andrews might be dead or alive by now. And, no wonder you kept saying the body temperature was a little off. A monkey's temperature is probably a little different than a human, but probably too close to see a noticeable difference."

"It's a whole new ballgame," Jim answered. "You get the chip and get back here. We've got a lot of work to do."

"Ok, We'll be there ASAP."

They met the two assistants at the Primate Research Lab. The assistants told them that the monkeys had come from an area around Kruger National Park and that Park ranges had been capturing monkeys for several weeks.

Jason remembered that their guides had commented on the several parked trucks and vans they had recently seen in the area. He also wondered how the chip got to South Africa. Was it in the monkey and the monkey was taken to Kruger Park, or was the chip brought to Kruger and placed in the monkey. It would probably take the FBI to find those answers and, at this point, his company was not in very good standing with any law enforcement agency. Hopefully all that would change with the new information they found. Thank God, the system does work, but they should never take anything for granted again.

Jason made arrangements to start scanning the monkeys with the Lab's X-ray equipment. They would start around 4:00 p.m. The staff at the Primate Lab was very cooperative. There were twelve monkeys delivered in the new shipment from Kruger Park, but it wouldn't take long even if they had to X-ray all of them.

Everything was set up for them. They started scanning monkeys and luck was with them. The seventh monkey had the chip. The Lab arranged for one of their research doctors to remove the chip and before six o'clock they were thanking the people at the lab and the president.

On the way to the Mobile airport Jason called Pete. Pete was stunned and found the story almost too unbelievable to be true. But, it did make sense and did explain why they could not find anything in the bush. He told Jason he would fly back to Indianapolis within the next couple days and that they would develop a new investigation plan.

At 8:45 that night Jason and Higgie were on a Delta flight back to Indianapolis with Harold Andrews' microchip in hand, tired as hell.

CHAPTER 13

NO CHIP, NO ANDREWS.

With the discovery of the microchip in a monkey, the trail of Harold Andrews became very cold. It was now up to law enforcement to find out if he was dead or alive. If alive, was he being held captive or did he play a part in his own disappearance? Did he embezzle 100 million dollars from his own company or was he kidnapped in order to use him to embezzle the money?

Jason felt somewhat responsible because his company was built on finding clients. He knew he was not responsible for the removal of Mr. Andrews' microchip. However, more precautions should have been taken to prevent the clients from having their microchips removed.

When Pete Donnelly arrived in Indianapolis, he, Jason, Higgie and Jim Kraft sat down to review where they were. Pete led the discussion.

"We have little to go on with what we found so far in upstate New York. We did not find any fingerprints on Mr. Andrews' car, which was quite unusual because someone had taken the time and effort to completely clean down the car. We think it was done before it was hidden. That would mean there is another crime location, somewhere where the car was located for an extended period of time. We can't say for sure that it was Andrews' hunting lodge but we really didn't find enough to say it wasn't."

He continued. "It is interesting that even though everyone

called his place a hunting lodge, there are little signs that other men hunted with him. When we brushed down the lodge for fingerprints we found a lot of different female prints and few male prints. The women's prints could have been from cleaning women. We did interview two different women who worked for Mr. Andrews on a part-time basis. Both women said that they had not been at the lodge for some time. Both also said that several other women had spent time at the lodge, but they did not know if it was business or pleasure. They do remember seeing other men in hunting outfits."

Higgie asked Pete, "Did anyone in the area remember seeing him just before he disappeared?"

Pete answered. "We did go to all the grocery stores, hardware stores, gas stations and hunting supply stores in the surrounding area. It seems that he kept to himself. There was one store, a combination food, supplies and gas station, about five miles from his lodge that had an old clerk who remembers Andrews. He said that Andrews was in the store during the week he disappeared, but he doesn't remember which day. Andrews paid cash. There wasn't any record of a credit card sale. His most interesting statement was that Andrews was driving a Volvo station wagon. We could find no records of his owning a Volvo. It may have been a rental but, if so, it wasn't rented anywhere around that area. His wife, Helen, says he did not own a Volvo. There is a Ford F-150 pickup at the lodge that he does own. It's still there."

Jason asked, "How many acres did he own, I suppose you went over the entire property?"

"We went over as much as we could. The lodge has four bedrooms and three baths. There are two outbuildings that house his truck, a tractor, a four-wheel Kawasaki mule, workshop, tools, and boating equipment. The lodge is a classic two-story, half-log, half-stone structure with a shake roof. It's huge, probably around five thousand square feet, so it's not your typical hunting lodge. It is full of antiques, fine art, tile floors, leather sofas, leather

chairs and has a modern kitchen. One room on the main level looks like a L.L. Bean store, everything you would need for hunting and fishing is in that room, including several duck mounts hanging on the walls. The property itself is around 300 acres and has a twenty-acre lake located a quarter mile from the lodge. The lake has a boat and fishing dock and duck blinds in four different locations. Duck hunters want a blind that faces with the wind so that ducks can fly towards the blind and set their wings into the wind for landing. He had blinds in several locations so he could always have a blind facing the right way, depending on the wind that day."

Pete paused and said, "Another theory is that Mr. Andrews may be located somewhere else in northern New York. There seemed to be a lot of activity involving his company during the days after his disappearance. I mean money disappearing and all. We think an operation like that would have to be done close range, meaning no more that a day's drive from New York City. We did find something of interest in the lodge. There were a lot of books, maps and travel guides for the Lake George area. That's not too far northeast from Andrews' lodge. It's right on Interstate 87 and a straight shot down to New York City."

Jason said, "I'm coming up to New York; I can't just sit around here and do nothing. How about I go up to Lake George and look around. I want to stop and see his hunting lodge anyway?"

Pete replied, "Tomorrow, Agent Henderson and I are going to New York to meet with Samuel Rome, at Andrews Investments. We didn't get the answers we were expecting the last time we were there. We'd like to try him again. If you'll give me a couple days, I'll go upstate with you."

Jason asked, "What answers did you expect from Mr.Rome?"

"Well, he seemed very evasive and was not real cooperative when we asked to review the company records. We talked to their Chief Financial Officer and he acted totally briefed on what to say. We discovered that Andrews made Rome a minority partner and that doesn't mean a black partner. If Rome has some ownership and the right of first refusal if anything happened to Mr. Andrews, that means he has the right to purchase Andrews shares, at a fair market price, before the company could be sold to anyone else. So, with Andrews out of the picture, Rome could be the Owner, President and the Chairman of the Board."

Higgie asked, "Did you find anything else in their records that would make you suspicious about him?"

"Yes, we found some other things that I can't discuss at this time. One thing I can tell you, because your company is involved, is that the five companies that invested in Pinpoint, Inc., were all dummy companies set up by Andrews Investments. One million dollars was deposited in each new company checking account and then a check was written and sent to you along with contracts and re-payment plans.

All this was done with five fake company names and regular post office boxes in five different cities. Rome denies knowing anything about the fake companies, but we don't believe him."

Jason said, "Ok, I'll bite. Why would Andrews Investments help me start my company? I don't see any benefit for them."

"Well, we don't know, but one theory is that whoever planned this might have known for a few years what they wanted to do. Having your microchip in a monkey, and us running around Africa chasing what we thought was Harold Andrews, gave someone a lot of time without the authorities snooping around New York City! Whoever it is really had all of us damn busy running around South Africa!"

"Then it probably was someone inside the company?" Jim Kraft said.

"Not necessarily," Pete answered. "Andrews International investing in Pinpoint, Inc., may not have anything to do with Mr. Andrews' disappearance. The information was too easy to get. Their records clearly show the investments. Nobody tried to cover it up. It's just that no one seems to know who set up the fake companies or approved them. Maybe Andrews just thought it was a good investment. There are way too many possibilities."

"So, what else can we do to help?" Jason offered.

"If you can't use a microchip to track Andrews, I'd say it's kind of up to us to find him. By the way, who would be qualified to remove a microchip, assuming they knew where it was?

Higgie answered, " If they didn't care about what happens to Andrews, anyone could. If they wanted to protect against things like gangrene, infections or never waking up, they would need a qualified doctor."

"Could I talk to your doctor who put his chip in, just to get a feel for the procedure? We know a little about this sort of thing, but you folks are on the cutting edge."

"Sure," Higgie answered. "However, the doctor who put the microchip in Mr. Andrews no longer works here. We had to let him go, but we have other doctors you can talk with."

"Why did you have to let him go?" Pete asked with a probing voice.

Jason said, "Well, it's a sad and tragic story. His name is Dr. Trammell Waller. He was part of our original team. I found out the reason he accepted our offer was for his wife to receive special medical treatments at the Indiana University Medical

Center for a disease called Non-Hodgkin's lymphoma. Not too long after we started implanting microchips, his wife died. It was a long, very difficult battle with cancer and it really took a toll on Trammell. He was drinking heavily before his wife's death, and afterwards he became a full blown alcoholic and lost all interest in life itself. He had some money, but his wife's illness pretty much drained most of the funds he had. Sadly, we just couldn't take a chance on his medical abilities and couldn't rely on his being sober, so we let him go."

"Where is he now?" Pete asked.

"We're not sure," Jason replied. "The last we heard of him, about six months ago, he was in a small apartment on the south side of Indianapolis, in an area called Southport. After he left, we never saw him again."

"Do you have his phone number or address?"

"Sure, I think so. We'll get it for you."

Pete added, "I'd still like to talk to one of your doctors. After I talk to Samuel Rome, I'll call you and let you know where we are. I know your company has a big stake in finding Harold Andrews."

After some small talk they invited Pete to dinner. He accepted and went back to the airport Holiday Inn to freshen up. Pete met them in the hotel lobby at seven o'clock. The dinner reservation was at the famous Chantéclair Restaurant which, surprisingly, was on the top floor of the Airport Holiday Inn Hotel. The Chantéclair, because of its unusual location, was known all over the Midwest. Small planes would fly in from Chicago just to eat there. It was not the cheapest place for a FBI agent to eat on a government expense account. However, Pinpoint, Inc. picked up the tab.

The next afternoon agents Pete and Jane arrived at Samuel

PINPOINT INC.

Rome's office. Lynn Pillow, the assistant, was there to greet them.

"Good afternoon, nice to see you again." Lynn said.

"Good afternoon to you too," Pete and Jane both replied.

"Mr. Rome is waiting for you. Please follow me."

Lynn took them into Mr. Rome's office. She didn't knock on his door. She just opened the door and walked right in.... again.

Rome stood and said, "Hello, you two, nice to see you again."

Pete thought to himself, It's really nice to meet important people who feel it's nice to see you. Or, is that just some New York bullshit?

"Nice to see you again, sir," Pete replied.

They all moved to the center of the office and took comfortable leather chairs in a semi-circle. It seemed a cozy and friendly way to talk.

Pete started the conversation. "Mr. Rome, who could have authorized the investment of five million dollars in the five fake companies that funded Pinpoint, Inc? As you know we discovered that fact the last time we were here."

Rome seemed a little taken back by the blunt question. It sounded like an accusation more than a question. "We have several people who are involved in our company's investment program. We also have an investment committee that meets every month. If our investments are not performing well, they meet more often. I checked and can find no record of the committee's approval of those investments."

"Does that mean that investments can be made without committee consent?" Pete asked.

Rome paused. "Usually at committee meetings, the committee makes recommendations, reviews current investments and monthly performance. They then make new proposals, change recommendations and pass all that information along to Mr. Andrews and myself."

"Does that mean Mr. Andrews or yourself can change or add any investments to the portfolio? Can either of you approve the portfolio, or do both of you have to approve?" Jane asked.

Rome now had a solemn, concerned look on his face. "Actually Mr. Andrews is to approve the investments. However, he usually leaves that up to me to review and approve for him. Of course I keep him totally up to date on a regular basis. He's a busy man and away from the office a lot."

Pete paused for the big question. "Did Mr. Andrews approve the establishing of the five fake companies and the million dollar deposit in each one?"

Now Rome was moving around in his chair looking for the right words to say. "Usually, I give Mr. Andrews the final recommendation from the committee and myself. He reviews and gives them back to me. Once they are approved, I give them to our Chief Financial Officer to implement."

"And with the five fake companies in question, Mr. Rome, did you recommend them to Mr. Andrews for his approval?" Pete asked.

"I don't remember these five companies ever being on any list, and I certainly didn't authorize the establishment of any fake companies or any funds for those companies." Rome's voice was cool, and stern, and also a little nervous.

"So, Mr. Andrews had to approve these companies without your knowledge?" Pete coolly replied.

"I just don't see how that's possible," Rome retorted.

"Well, it was done, Mr. Rome. So it's possible," Pete said with a smile.

"Can I speak again with your Chief Financial Officer?"

"Why certainly. I will arrange it. He's not here today. He's at a seminar in Boston, but he'll be back in a couple of days."

"Thank you, I need to talk to him as soon as possible."

Pete continued. "On another subject, I assume you have not been contacted by anyone in regards to Mr. Andrews' disappearance."

"Of course not, I would tell you if someone had contacted me," Rome snapped back, with a shaken voice.

"Has Mrs. Andrews contacted you about her husband?" Jane asked.

"Why yes, of course. She and I talk regularly. With her husband gone, I discuss all company affairs with her."

Pete replied, "I thought she had nothing to do with the company. It is our understanding she was not involved in his business life at all."

Rome, now twitching a bit, readjusted his position in his chair, crossed his legs and said, "She hasn't been involved in the business at all until now. She called and told me she was going to become more involved and was assuming her husband's position until he was found. I've met with our legal people and they told me there's nothing I could do but agree, at least at this time."

"If Mr. Andrews is not found, or found dead, can she assume her husband's assets of the company, or does your right of first refusal agreement give you the right to override her decision and force her to sell her husbands interest?"

"My God, man, what are you getting to? Are you accusing me of being involved in Harold Andrews' disappearance?" Rome's voice was now just below a roar and becoming unpleasant.

"No, No Mr. Rome. We just need to understand everything involving the company. Our job is to develop every scenario possible, even the ones that may not make sense." Pete was trying to sooth Samuel's nerves and manner.

"If I am a suspect, I want to know."

"Mr. Rome, you are no more a suspect than anyone else in your company or at Pinpoint, Inc. Until we have more to go on, everyone will be considered, "Pete said with firmness.

"Is there anything else?" Rome said with a sharp tone.

"Not for now, Mr. Rome. If you'll be so kind to let us know when your Chief Financial Office is available, we'd appreciate it"

"Of course, Lynn will let you know." Rome offered his hand as he rose from his chair, signaling that the meeting was over.

They all shook hands and Pete and Jane left. Pete and Jane went back to their office to follow up background information involving Dr. Trammell Wells, Samuel Rome and the Chief Financial Officer. They also had to figure out how the monkey and the chip got to Kruger Park. Then there was Helen Andrews and the five fake companies that funded Pinpoint, Inc. They were not without things to do.

At Pinpoint, Inc. a dilemma was occurring. After spending several nights together, Jason and Higgie were torn between an open office romance or keeping a secret office affair. Ever since their return from South Africa they took turns visiting each other's homes in the evenings. Sometimes the visit lasted the night. The relationship may have started with a physical attraction, but they were now bordering on a solid love affair. They just looked great together. He was the tall, handsome, an up-and coming entrepreneur with pretty blue eyes and a great smile. She was the intelligent, good-looking, blue-eyed microchip expert that had his heart and his hormones in a titter. All in all, they were perfect together.

PINPOINT INC.

The next day Jason and Higgie drove to Southport, just south of Indianapolis, hoping to find Dr. Trammel Waller. They were surprised to find that his house was a one-story, brick, unkempt and overgrown mess. There was no car in the drive and empty trashcans on the curb. They checked his freestanding mailbox and found that it was full of unsolicited advertisements. They also found his light and gas bill, along with the water bill. Sure signs he had not been home in some time.

After checking the front and back door and finding them locked, they went to the neighbor's house.

An older, white-headed black woman in her seventies came to the door.

"Whatcha want!" she said with a slight tone of being interrupted.

"Hello, Ma'am. My name is Jason Higgins and this is Paula Higginbothem. We are associates of Dr. Waller and were wondering if you knew where he is."

"He don't tell me nothing, ain't my business," she said.

"Do you know if he has been gone long?" Higgie said, hoping a woman could communicate better than a white male.

"Don't know. He ain't lived there for but seven months. Came with his wife, but she passed right after they got themselves in." "Would anyone know where he might be?" Jason asked.

"Don't know. He got that new car a few weeks ago and I ain't seen him since."

"Oh, he got a new car." Jason answered.

"Yep, a pretty blue one; I don't know if it was really new, but it sure looked good to me! Real uptown looking, you know what I mean?"

Jason smiled. "Thank you. Here is my card. If Dr. Waller returns home would you give me a call? If you call, I'll even come out and bring you some fresh flowers or something for being so nice to call."

"Aren't you just sweet. Sure, I'll be calling. What kinda flowers you gonna bring?"

"You tell me what kind you want when you call, and I'll bring them."

"Sure enough!" she exclaimed.

They got back in their car and drove back to Pinpoint, Inc. Along the way they talked about Trammell Waller being gone for so long. They wondered if he had any family. Could he be staying with family or friends? Their records unfortunately did not ask about other family members.

While in the car Jason called Clinton Byron, the FBI agent in Indianapolis Pete had brought to meet Jason. When Clinton answered, Jason asked him to contact the local power and water company and put a flag on Dr. Waller's accounts. He thought Waller might try to contact these companies to pay his bills or close his account. If he does that, the postmark could tell where he is. Then again he may not give a crap about paying bills or closing accounts.

After Jason hung up from agent Clinton Byron, Higgie said, "Oh boy, that's a long shot! I hope we're not going to sit around here and wait for that to happen!"

"Ok, Miss Brainpower, come up with something better."

"Ok, how about this? We hire a private eye to find him for us."

"Well, hell, that's too easy!" Jason said with a laugh as he punched her playfully on the shoulder. "That's cheat'in! Besides, we got the FBI."

When they returned to the office, Jason asked a secretary at Pinpoint to call a staff meeting for nine o'clock the next morning. They had to figure out something to do, and they had to do it quickly. He spent the rest of the day thinking about different directions to take. He also pondered what he was going to do about his covert office affair. At least covert to everyone except Jim, who knew what was going on, but also knew where his bread was buttered and would kept his mouth shut.

At the staff meeting the next morning Jason briefed everyone on what had happened since Harold Andrews disappeared. He said, "Let's open up our minds, think like Harold Andrews or think like his capturers. If they kidnapped him, how would they pull off stealing 100 million dollars? If he plotted his own disappearance, how would he pull it off? Is the missing money the only answer for his disappearance? If he did it himself, did he need someone else to help him? Do we all agree that the chip in a monkey in South Africa was just to throw off the authorities? Would capturers just kill him after they got what they wanted or would they try to ransom him? Is it an inside job or an outside job?"

He stopped, looked around the room and said, "OK, kids, let's come up with some ideas. There may be bonuses involved!"

That afternoon Pete called from New York.

"Jason, I think we have a break. We contacted Delta and asked them to run a check on Dr. Trammell Waller for the two weeks prior to Andrews' disappearance and, bingo, Waller flew from Indianapolis to Atlanta to Johannesburg five days before the disappearance. He had to fly under his own name because of his passport. He was there three days and flew back to Atlanta and then to Sarasota Florida. It sure looks like he's our guy who planted the chip in the monkey."

"That's great Pete. Do we know if Andrews was involved with Dr. Waller?"

"No, we don't know why Dr. Waller did what he did. It still could be for someone else rather than Andrews."

"What now?" Jason asked.

We have contacted our agents in the Sarasota area and they are looking for Waller. It shouldn't be to hard find him if he has rented or bought anything there. I will fly to Sarasota as soon as they have him."

"I'll go with you. He worked for me and I need to know what happened with our chip."

"I guess that would be ok since you're a Junior G-man," Pete quipped.

"Well, I didn't shoot myself in my leg or my ass, did I?"

Pete cut the conversation short. "I've got to hang up. I'll call you as soon as we hear from Sarasota."

The fact that Dr. Trammell Waller was involved with the Andrews case was the buzz of the Pinpoint, Inc. office. Theories flew and comments about the Monkey Doctor abounded.

In Sarasota, the local authorities were moving in on Dr. Waller. They had discovered that his current address was on Midnight Pass in Siesta Key. When they went to the house, he wasn't home. So they staked it out.

That evening Jason was on his way home after having dinner with the local FBI agent, Clinton Byron. They had discussed the case and agreed to stay in close touch. Clinton was interested in the involvement of Dr. Waller.

It was around ten o'clock and as Jason pulled into his driveway he noticed a black four-door sedan sitting across the street. His home was on a quiet, wooded street in a residential neighborhood. Not the place a car would be parked at ten o'clock at night.

As Jason raised his garage door from inside his car, the inside lights came on inside the parked car across the street.

Both front car doors opened and two men walked across the street towards Jason's house. Jason acted like he didn't see the men and closed the garage door and went from inside the garage into the house.

His front doorbell rang and he became very tense and unsure of what to do. His first thought was that it was the FBI or other authorities. It was the only thing that made sense. He yelled, "Just a minute" to the men on the front porch. He then called Higgie and told her that two men were at the front door and just to be safe, he would lay the open phone line on the table so she could hear everything. He laid the phone down.

As he opened the door, the two men moved close so they could talk quietly. They were dark-skinned, but not black. They both had dark hair, dark eyes and half-grown beards. One man spoke with an obvious Middle East accent.

"Good evening, Mr. Higgins. Sorry to bother you so late."

Jason cautiously said, "What can I do for you?"

"May we come in?" one of the men said.

"I think it's a little late. Can we discuss whatever it is tomorrow?" Jason said.

"No, I don't think so, Mr. Higgins!" the man said in a quiet, stern voice.

"What is this about?" Jason said loudly.

"We need to locate Mr. Harold Andrews and we understand you and your company may know where he is."

"No, I don't know where he is. Can I ask who you are?"

The one man, who had been talking, replied, "My name is Abdul. I I am visiting your country from Saudi Arabia. It is necessary for my company and my government to talk to Mr. Andrews."

"Well, I'm sorry. We do not know where Mr. Andrews is.

We are also looking for him," Jason said in a loud voice hoping Higgie could hear him over the phone.

"We would like to ask for your cooperation. We are very serious about finding Mr. Andrews," the man said softly and very firmly.

"Have you talked to the authorities?" Jason asked.

"No, no, Mr Higgins, we must do this ourselves."

"I'm sorry. There is nothing I can tell you," Jason said in a loud, strong voice that could easily be heard on the phone.

The man leaned forward, looked straight into Jason's eyes and said,

"It would be in your best interest to help us. We are not the only ones looking for Mr. Andrews. It would be a mistake for you not to cooperate with us."

"Can I ask what you want with Harold Andrews? I'm just curious."

"I can tell you that my country has lost investments in Mr. Andrews' company and that those investments must be returned."

"I can't help you because I do not know where Mr. Andrews is. I would like to know, but I don't," Jason said, hoping that would end the conversation.

"We will not stop until we find Mr. Andrews. We will be in contact with you again. We expect you to cooperate with us. We would suggest that you do not tell the authorities about this visit. Is this understood?"

"Are you threatening me?" Jason said.

"Oh no, Mr.Higgins, it is not a threat. We are only asking for cooperation to find someone we are both looking for."

Jason stepped back from the front door and said, "Thank you and good night." He closed the door thinking to himself how stupid it was to say thank you and good night. Why would I be thanking them, hell, they scared the begeebees out of me!

He watched through the front window and saw the two men return to their car and drive off. He went back to the open phone on the table.

"Did you hear that? They wanted info on Harold Andrews. They were from Saudi Arabia! They did not seem like nice men."

"I only heard a little of it, mostly you talking loud! I couldn't hear much of what they said."

"I could tell they were talking softly so the neighbors wouldn't hear." Jason said, "I wouldn't let them in the house, so, we stood outside the front door."

"Were they nice?" she said.

"Were they nice?" Jason said, half yelling. "They threatened me. I wouldn't call that very nice."

"Threatened you with what?" she said.

"I don't know, just threatened me."

"Maybe they'll stay away," Higgie said softly.

"Don't bet on it. They sounded very serious to me. They said something about other people looking for Andrews. I better call Pete and Clinton Byron tomorrow as I may need them. I don't do well with Middle Eastern guys."

They talked for a few more moments about getting together the next evening and then said goodnight.

The first thing the next morning Jason called Pete and told him the entire story about the visit from the Saudi guys. Pete was interested in the fact that other OPEC countries were also looking. He asked if Jason got their license number.

"Hell no, I didn't take one step out of my house. It didn't look too safe to me at the time. They weren't there to play. Where do you think they will look for Andrews?"

"My guess it would be in New York City and upper state around his lodge. We did finally get that information from the Chief Financial Officer at the Andrews' company. Saudi Arabia was one of the countries that lost 20 million."

"20 million, wow, who else lost?" Jason exclaimed.

"There were five countries, each losing 20 million: Venezuela, Indonesia, Iran, Saudi Arabia and United Arab Emirates. These five were among the largest investors in the company and they moved most of the money through electronic transactions.

Jason said in a thoughtful tone, "So now we got the FBI, local and state authorities, the press, thugs from five OPEC countries and Pinpoint, Inc., all looking for the one and only Mr. Harold Andrews?"

"Yea, and I hope we find him first or he may not be able to talk to us when we do find him," Pete muttered.

"Any word on Dr. Waller?" Jason asked.

"Not yet. But I'll let you know as soon as we make contact. Got to go. Keep safe and don't do anything dumb and don't be a hero."

"What the hell does that mean?" Jason asked.

"Just what it says, think before you act with these Middle-East guys."

Jason took a really deep breath. "Oh! Now I really feel great! Why don't you just come and beat them up for me?"

"I think it's a little late for that," Pete chuckled.

"Go to hell, G-Man!"

"After you, my boy, after you."

Jason called Clinton Byron and told the story again. Clinton told Jason he was there twenty-four hours a day for him. Jason was happy to know that he had backup in case the bad guys came around again. They chatted for a few more minutes, then said goodbye.

Higgie and Jason had just finished a large sausage and onion pizza when the phone rang at Jason's home. It was Pete.

"We still can't find Dr. Waller. He didn't come home and our guys are still staked out waiting for him. I'm not going down there until he shows up. We also found out that your Dr. Waller flew to Little Rock the week before he flew to South Africa. We checked all the hotels in the area and he didn't stay at any of them. He flew back to Indianapolis the next afternoon. As I said, that was six days before he flew to Atlanta and then to Johannesburg."

Jason said, "Does any of that make any sense to you? It sounds like he stayed with someone he obviously knows."

"No it doesn't make any sense. But we don't know who he was meeting in Little Rock. It may or may not have been Andrews. I can't imagine he went there for a one day vacation."

"Interesting," Jason said. "That's about the same time his neighbor in Southport told me he showed up in a new blue car. Maybe he came into some cash while in Little Rock."

"We'll know when we catch up with him. He's got to come home sooner or later. The fact that it's another rental house also means that he can just skip out again, you never know. Another interesting fact is that Samuel Rome has hired a lawyer to talk to us. He evidently doesn't want to answer our questions directly. I think he's feeling some pressure. I also understand he might be getting some heat from the Middle East countries that are missing a lot of money. His financial officer did say that they were getting a lot of uncomfortable calls from clients. Maybe good ole Samuel will need us to protect him from his own clients."

"So, what's your schedule?" Jason asked Pete. "I want to come up."

"Give me one more day and fly into LaGuardia. I'll pick you up," Pete said.

"Ok, can you get me a hotel room for one night and then I'll go up to Lake George. Charge it to my company."

"Sure, how much can you afford? The "Y" is fifty bucks and the Plaza is five hundred. Which one ya want?"

"Any other choices?" Jason replied with a chuckle.

"Yea, we get a good rate at the Crowne Plaza. It's on Broadway, right in the middle of all the action! Not that you need any more action than you already have!"

"Action? I'm not getting any action. I need action! The Crowne Plaza sounds good to me. Put me there. I'll let you know my arrival time as soon as I can get it set up."

They exchanged a couple more joking barbs and said goodbye.

Two days later, Jason's plane landed at LaGuardia airport in New York. Pete was at the luggage carousel to pick up Jason. They shook hands and he drove Jason downtown to the Manhattan Crowne Plaza at 49th and Broadway.

They had dinner that night and Pete briefed Jason on all the current information they had discovered. One of the hot, new discoveries was that Helen Andrews withdrew $150,000 from her personal account three weeks before Harold disappeared.

Jason said, "That doesn't sound good. Maybe she paid someone to move him out of the picture."

"She told us that Harold had asked her to take $150,000 out of their house account so he could deposit it in a bank close to his lodge. She said his plan was to put some kind of addition or upgrade on his hunting lodge.

"They had $150,000 in a house account!" Jason exclaimed.

"She says that he put it in the account the month before and told her to get it out because he was busy doing something else."

"Yea, right!" Jason snapped back. "And I don't suppose there is any trace of where the money is now."

"Of course not, she says she has no idea what he did with it."

"Ok, now we have three hot suspects, Rome, Helen and Harold." Jason said.

"Actually, we have four. Don't forget that Dr. Waller has been doing some really strange things."

Jason replied, "I can't imagine that Waller is smart enough or in any mental condition to do something like this. He wouldn't go after fifty million dollars. He'd settle for one million, just to keep himself in booze. So what do we do now, G-man?"

"We keep looking. We're going to dig deeper into the $150,000 withdraw from the house account and whether or not Rome has been out of the city in recent weeks. What's your plan for tomorrow?"

"I'm renting a car and going north. Can you give me some directions?"

"Sure, come to my office first and we'll help you find a rental car, charge it to your company and get you some directions."

"Pete, I've got your address at the FBI office. I'll take a cab and be at your office at 9:00 a.m. You will be up by then, won't you?"

"We do more, before 9 a.m. than most people do in a day!"

"Oh sure, I saw that commercial, didn't believe the Army either."

Pete dropped Jason off at the hotel after dinner. He stopped at the lobby bar and had a Grey Goose martini. After thirty minutes he thought about taking a walk outside the hotel, but realized it would be like taking a walk around Londolozi, only with different animals. Common sense won out and he went to bed, by himself.

CHAPTER 14

UPSTATE NEW YORK

It was 9:00 a.m. when Jason walked into Pete's office.

"OK, G-Man, its 9 a.m. Show me what you've done before 9 a.m. that the rest of us normal people can't do, and don't include drinking several cups of coffee and eating a dozen donuts."

"Well, for your information, smarty pants, we've found out a few things that you'll find interesting."

Jason sat down across the desk from Pete, smiled, took a deep breath and said, "Lay it on me."

Well, for starters, our number two man at Andrews International, Mr. Samuel Rome, owns an apartment just a few blocks from his office."

Jason, looking bored, leaned back in his chair and quipped, "Wow, that's really hot news, I wonder how many executives in New York own apartments close to their office."

Pete cocked his head with a puckered smile and replied, "Probably many. However, how many do you think have the lovely, socialite wife, Helen Andrews, spend a few nights?"

"What!" exclaimed Jason, "No-way!"

"Hello there! We have a doorman who says Helen Andrews has spent several nights there, and maybe a few afternoons. And, we know that Samuel has been there at the same time, maybe as an employee consulting with the boss' wife or maybe even playing a little strip dominos."

Jason was frozen in time. "Let me get this straight. Helen,

the stuffy wife, and Samuel, the heir to the corporate throne, has been reviewing his corporate benefits package, while good ole Harold disappears along with one hundred million of the corporate funds. Gee, I'm no Rhodes Scholar, but that seems a little too convenient."

"Wait a minute, Sherlock," Pete interrupted, "There's more strange stuff."

"Oh, swell," Jason moaned.

"Remember Gordon Dunbar, the strange ole fart who found Andrews'car? It turns out that nobody in the county knows who he is.

When good ole Deputy Frank Barns did the investigation, it seems that he forgot to get Dunbar's address and phone number. Let's just say that Deputy Frank wasn't the sharpest crayon in the box. We've searched all the records for phone numbers, taxes, land deeds and titles, and there's no Gordon Dunbar. Even sheriff Frey says he has no idea who he might be."

Jason thought for a second. "I thought he said he owned the land where the car was found."

"Ok, Dumbo, open your ears. There's no record of Dunbar. We located the land owner, who is a very old farmer, and he has owned that land for years and has never heard of Dunbar."

"Any more good news, G-man?"

Pete was enjoying this give and take. "Oh sure, what do you want first, the kind of good news or the not so good news?"

"This is not sounding like more good news," Jason sighed.

"You bet your sweet ass this isn't good news. It turns out that our good sheriff, Ken Frey, was well acquainted with Harold Andrews. In fact, he hunted ducks at Andrews' lodge on several occasions. After checking phone records we discovered that Andrews called the Sheriff a week before he disappeared. Sheriff Frey says it was just an invitation to hunt."

"Oh, Christ, stop the bleeding!" Jason moaned again.

"Oh, don't get the band-aid yet, Hoosier. There's more."

"We've checked for all types of law enforcement meetings in Albany for the days the sheriff was gone and we found zilch.... nadda.... nothing.

However, our good ole sheriff now says that he went to attend a meeting and that it was cancelled after he arrived in Albany. He says that he decided to take the week off and go to his family farm in Lake George."

Jason frowned. "So, what do you think? Is he telling the truth?"

"Well, don't you find it strange that he was conveniently out of Jasper when the now unknown Gordon Dunbar appeared out of nowhere with his fake stories about owning the land and about finding the car. And, by the way, isn't it convenient that a sharp, trained officer like Barney Fife, oh sorry, I meant Frank Barns, was the only person in town to handle the entire investigation?"

Jason's mind was now whirling with wild thoughts. "I hope you don't have any more good news to share with me. I think my inbox is full."

"Well, now you know what we do before 9:00 a.m. Let's go down to the coffee shop and have those several cups of coffee and those dozen donuts. I'm sure you'll want to hear the other goodies I've got for you."

Needing a break, Jason replied, "Only if the news is actually good news. I've had all the surprises I need before my second cup of caffeine."

Nothing about the case was spoken on the way to the coffee shop. Pete let Jason digest the early morning news before he went on to the noontime edition.

During the snack break, Pete asked Jason what he was going to do while in Lake George or at Andrews' hunting lodge.

Jason wasn't real sure. "Hell, I have no idea what I'm looking for but I've got to do something to help. I can't just sit in Indianapolis and do nothing."

"We've been to Lake George, Jason, and we didn't find anything. However, at that time we didn't know that Sheriff Frey had a family farm there. Maybe we do need to check that out. Tell you what, my friend, you wait until this afternoon and I'll drive up with you. Maybe we should also take another look at Andrews' lodge. I still think there's something there we've missed."

Pete called agent Jane Henderson. He asked her to take over the day-to-day responsibilities of the Andrews' case. He then told Jason, "OK, you go back to your hotel and I'll pick you up around 2:30 this afternoon and don't get lost."

"Very funny. Do you think I can make it back, by cab, all by myself?"

"Well, I could always get someone from my office to go with you," Jake said, in baby talk, with a big grin.

Jason gave Pete a glare. "Is it appropriate to say go to hell, asshole, in a federal building?"

Jason took a cab back to his hotel, called his office and asked for Higgie. She answered.

"Hi there, good looking. I know you're just in deep depression without my warm, athletic body to wrap your arms around."

"Actually, I have my hands wrapped around a Danish and am enjoying a wonderful cup of coffee. What did you say your name was?"

"Very funny. I suppose you also went out on a date last night and had a wonderful time."

"More than a wonderful time, I'm actually totally exhausted this morning, must have been awake and active most of the night."

"Ok, goodbye. I'll call you when you're not too tired to talk."

"What did you say your name was?" Higgie laughed.

"Well, no wonder I haven't asked you to marry me. You can be a real bitch sometimes."

"Of course, and you love every bitchy minute."

"Ok,ok uncle, playtime is over. Anything happening there?"

"Nope, we are still trying to find more information on Dr.Waller, but can't find a trace of him anywhere around Indianapolis. It looks like after he went down to Sarasota, he never came back here."

"Have you talked to Agent Byron in the FBI office there since I left?"

"Yes, and they haven't had any signs of Waller in Sarasota. They assume that since the airlines have no records of him flying out of there, he must have driven out."

"That means he could be anywhere," Jason groaned.

"Are you going to northern New York? Everything seems to be leaning to that area," she said.

"Do you think Waller would go there? Hell, I don't know. Maybe he went back to South Africa to find his pet monkey."

"So, what are you gonna do?"

"Pete and I are driving up to Lake George and to the Andrews' lodge later this afternoon to see if we missed anything. I suppose G-Man Pete will have some ideas, maybe car rentals, hotels or things like that."

"I don't think Andrews or Waller would use their own name renting anything, do you?"

"You're being way too practical. I like playing long shots, and this is sure one of them," he answered with a little sarcasm.

Higgie went into her special, sexy voice for him. "Ok,

sweetheart, I'll lay awake all night and think of your wonderful warm, athletic body and yearn for your return."

"Ah Jez, don't do that," Jake moaned. "It's hard enough being away without that lovey-dovey stuff. Put yourself in a zip lock bag until I get home."

"You got it, tiger. Be safe. Love ya!"

At 2:45 p.m. Jason was in the hotel lobby waiting for Pete. He noticed a couple of guys sitting across from the front desk staring at him. He thought they looked familiar. Were they the Mid-East guys that came to his home that night and scared the hell out of him? He just couldn't tell for sure and he wasn't about to go ask. He crossed the main lobby and went out the front door to the street. Sure enough, the two guys got up and walked to the front window.

Oh shit, he said to himself. Where the hell is Pete?

He stood on the sidewalk, looking around at the buildings as if he was a tourist in New York for the first time. It was the only thing he could think of doing to look unconcerned. Just then Pete pulled up to the curb. Jason opened the passenger door and said, "It's the guys from my house in Indianapolis."

"What the hell you talking about?" Pete exclaimed.

"You know, the Mid-East guys that came to my house looking for Andrews——the ones who told me they had better find him or else."

Pete looked over Jason's shoulder and saw nobody. "Where are they now?

Jason, without looking back said, "Right there in the main window."

"I don't see anyone in the main window. Are you sure it's them?"

"Hell no, but they sure were interested in me, and when I

went to the front door they both got up and came to the window to see where I was going."

Pete put the car in park and turned off the key. He got out and started walking swiftly towards the hotel front door. Jason followed.

"Geeze Pete, you got a gun or something with you?"

"Take it easy Jason, we're just walking to the front door. We're not storming the building."

"Yea, but what if they are still there?"

"So, they're still there. We act like we don't even see them and walk to the front desk."

"What do we do at the front desk?"

"You ask if you have any messages."

When they went through the front door and saw nothing of the two men in question, they walked to the front desk. Jason asked if he had any messages.

"Yes sir, Mr. Higgins." The desk clerk went to his room box and pulled out a message and handed it to Jason. The message read, "Mr. Higgins, we are waiting to hear where Mr. Andrews is located. We will not wait much longer. Either you or Mr. Rome must tell us. Our government is very unhappy. We will be in contact." Jason had a chill run up his spine. He handed the message to Pete who turned around and walked to the gift shop, bought a newspaper, peered around the lobby and motioned to Jason to head for the front door.

When they were in the car Pete said, "Well, I guess they were the same guys and they didn't want to be seen. I really don't like this. They could become a little nasty."

Jason stared at Pete and said, "Oh swell, I'm busting my butt to find Andrews and save my company and these guys want to take it out on me."

"So, you want me to give you my gun, or something?"

"Hey, Pete, it's not funny."

"I know. Sorry, but you know they're looking for Andrews. They're not after you. Why would they harm you?"

"If they think I know something, or have a lead, they may want to get it out of me and that could cause pain."

"This is true," Pete sighed.

Pete called his office and asked for someone to check out the hotel for a couple of Mid-East guys. He asked that they call him if they actually found anyone staying there or hanging around with that description.

On the way to Lake George they talked about possible theories in the case. They talked about motives and what someone would do with one hundred million dollars. Obviously the money would be hidden in Swiss bank accounts, so the possibility of finding the money being moved was a pipedream.

The difficultly in putting theories together was that they didn't actually know who the bad guy or guys were. Was Andrews alive or dead? Was Andrews the brains or simply an expendable pawn in a big money chess game? They had to find a break in the case, something that could point them in the right direction. Who was doing what?

Upon reaching Lake George they drove straight to the sheriff's office, where Pete had earlier discussed the case with several local officers. The first break happened when they entered the office.

Ed Hill, one of the deputies, saw Pete and immediately started his report on the latest findings. "We have covered all the rental agencies and hotels, looking for any names that might be connected, but with no luck. However, we put some names into our regional computer, and guess who was given a warning ticket, for speeding, a few days before Andrews disappeared?"

Pete said, "I have no earthly idea. Go ahead, make my day."

The officer grinned and answered, "How about the honorable Dr. Trammell Waller."

Pete looked stunned. "You've got to be kidding. That idiot has the entire law enforcement community looking for him, and he gets picked up for speeding? So, what address did he give?"

"The address was a house in Sarasota Florida. Unfortunately, at the time, we weren't looking for him," the officer replied.

"That's ok," Pete said with a big smile. "At least we know that Dr. Waller is in the game, regardless of who the boss is."

"What if Waller is the boss?" Jason said.

Pete gave Jason a killer look and said, "I don't think he would have the

brains or the financial backing to pull off a big hit like this."

Jason retorted, "Well, he was smart enough to have all of us running around like fools in South Africa while millions of dollars were stolen in New Your City." He thought for a moment and added, "You don't suppose

that Dr. Waller and the mysterious Gordon Dunbar are the same person, do you?"

Pete looked puzzled. "I don't think so, because the physical descriptions didn't sound the same, but what do I know? Could it have been Andrews himself? Let's get Andrews' picture and let Deputy Frank Barns take a look at it."

Pete called his office and asked them to get Andrew's picture and send it to the Sheriff's office in Lake George. Meanwhile, they interviewed the officer who stopped Trammell Waller for speeding. The officer could remember little because it was just a routine stop at the time.

It was now late afternoon. Pete and Jason checked into the Lake George Holiday Inn. They had a drink, a great dinner, and called it quits for the evening.

CHAPTER 15

THE STORY UNFOLDS

The next morning Pete and Jason went back to the Lake George Sheriff's office. The picture of Andrews arrived and they headed for Jasper to talk to Deputy Barns.

When they arrived in Jasper, Deputy Barns was at his desk, in the rear of the darkened room. This time he appeared to be awake.

"What can I do for you today?" blurted out the deputy.

"We met before. I'm agent Pete Donnelly and this is Jason Higgins."

"Oh, yes sir," Replied Barns; so impressed to be talking to a FBI agent, he forgot to even look at Jason. "I'm real glad to see you again. Are you still working on that case involving that car I found?"

"Yes we are," replied Pete. "I'd like for you to look at this picture and tell me if this might be the man who told you he was Gordon Dunbar."

He showed Barns the picture of Andrews.

"No sir," replied Barns. "That's not Gordon Dunbar. It don't look anything like him. I'd remember him, if I saw him again."

Pete asked, "Is Sheriff Frey in?"

"Yes sir, he is. He's over at the court house, but I expect him back at any minute. Want me to call over there and tell him you're here?"

"That would be very nice," replied Pete.

Barnes made the call and Sheriff Frey said he'd be right there.

When Sheriff Frey walked in, Pete and Jason were standing near the front door. He nodded at Jason and shook hands with Pete.

Looking directly at Pete, the sheriff asked, "What can I do for you?"

"Well, sheriff, I want you to meet Jason Higgins. He owns a company in Indianapolis. His company is involved in the Andrews case."

After Jason and sheriff Frey shook hands, Pete continued, "I understand you have a farm in Lake George and you were there for a week or so, not too long ago."

"That's right. I had gone up to Albany for a meeting and it was cancelled, so I went up to my family farm for a few days. It's only about an hour from Albany."

"Do you have someone taking care of the farm when you're not there?"

"Sure, his name is David Short. He leases most of the land for cattle range. He also maintains the land and the farmhouse."

"Does he live in the farmhouse?" asked Jason.

"No, he lives a few miles down the road."

"Anything else you would like to tell us about your relationship with Harold Andrews?"

"Nope, we were just friends who enjoyed duck hunting."

Pete was not quite happy with that answer, but replied,

"Thanks for you time, Sheriff. Hope to see you again soon." The Sheriff smiled and shook their hands.

They got back into their car and headed towards the Andrews hunting lodge.

"Well, what do you think?" Pete asked Jason.

"I have no idea. I was hoping Andrews was Gordon Dunbar."

"There's just something about Sheriff Frey that rubs me the wrong way," Jake answered. "He just doesn't seem to be telling us everything he knows, and I can't figure out why."

"I feel the same way. I say we go to the Frey farm and talk to the caretaker, David Short."

"Good idea, but first let's go to the Andrews lodge and take another look."

They drove to the hunting lodge and parked in front of the main house.

Pete suggested that they take another look in the outbuildings. After a half hour of walking around, finding nothing new, they started back to the main lodge. A car drove into the driveway and pulled up behind Pete's car. A woman, dressed in working clothes, in her fifties, got out and walked over to Pete and Jason.

"Can I help you gentlemen?" the lady said.

"Hello, I'm FBI agent Pete Donnelly and this is Jason Higgins, and you are?"

"Shirley Hart," she stated firmly.

Pete continued, "Shirley, we are here reviewing our notes on Mr. Andrews' disappearance. We were hoping to find something that would give us some idea of what might have happened to him."

"Well, Mr. Donnelly. I really haven't seen him in a few weeks. I'm not really sure he was here just before he disappeared. I told that to the other agents when they were here several days ago. I just come in and clean the place, and I'm still on my schedule. I'm also hoping that someone will get me caught up on my back pay."

"When was the last time you saw Mr. Andrews?" Pete asked.

"He had a bunch of guys up to hunt not too long ago, maybe three or four weeks ago."

"Was Sheriff Frey, from Jasper, here?"

"Why sure he was. He's here a lot."

"Did you know any of the other men?"

"Not by name, but some of them have been here before. There's a picture in one of the bedrooms of some men who have been here before and a couple of them in the picture were here on the last hunt."

"Can you show us that picture?"

"Sure, come with me." She led them to an upstairs bedroom and a picture on the nightstand of several men holding a lot of dead ducks.

"I think these two men were here," pointing to a couple of guys standing together. "I think they came with Sheriff Frey. That's Sheriff Frey right there next to them."

"Thank you, I'm going to take this picture, but it will be returned."

"Whatever you say, Mr. Donnelly."

They returned to the car and headed towards Lake George. When they arrived they returned to the sheriff's office. They asked for help locating Sheriff Frey's family farm. The local agents had the information in a matter of minutes. They drove out to the farm.

When they arrived, nobody was in the farmhouse or around the area. They proceeded to check all the outbuildings and peer into the house through the windows. Pete called back to the sheriff's office and asked to find the phone number and address of the caretaker, David Short. After getting the number and address, he called David Short. There was no answer. They drove to the address, which was not far away.

Driving up a long gravel drive to David Short's property, they noticed a pick up truck parked in front of one of the outbuildings. It was about seventy-five yards from the main house. After knocking on the front door, with no response, they drove towards the pick up truck. As they got out of their car, a man opened the door of the outbuilding and walked towards their car.

"Hi ya there," the man yelled, with a deep voice.

"Hello;" Pete said.

"What can I do for ya?" the man said.

"Are you David Short?"

"Sure am, was yesterday and will be tomorrow."

Pete introduced himself and Jason. "Well, Mr. Short, I was wondering if you could give me some information about Sheriff Frey. We are investigating a case and we are concerned that the sheriff might be in some danger. Some of the evidence in this case was found in his county, around Jasper, and some dangerous people are demanding information."

"You talking about that rich guy from New York City that disappeared?

"Yes, that's the case."

"Yea, the sheriff was friends with that guy. They went duck hunting together over at that guy's lodge. I think the whole family was friends with him."

"What do you mean the whole family?" Pete asked with slight quickness in his voice.

"Frey's brothers, they were all friends."

"How many brothers does the sheriff have?"

"He has two brothers. They come up to hunt with Sheriff Frey."

"And where do the two brothers live?"

"Oh, I'm not real sure. I think one lives in Florida and the other one lives somewhere else in the south. I pick them up at the airport sometimes. I'm not sure where they come from. I just meet them at the baggage pickup."

Pete went back to his car and retrieved the hunting picture from the lodge and showed it to Short. "Are the two brothers in this picture?"

"Sure, that's them right there next to the sheriff. None of them look alike, but they're all brothers."

"And they were here recently?"

"Yep, they were here all week a few weeks ago," Short replied.

"Any chance we might look around the farm? We'd like to get a feel for what a working cattle farm is really like. We boys from the city don't get much chance to actually visit a farm," Pete said cautiously.

"Why, I don't see why not. Help yourself. I've got to check a couple of fences and get ready to do some feeding, but you can go on and look all you want."

"Thanks, we'll probably get a chance to talk to you again soon," Pete said.

"No problem," Short replied and waved to them as they walked towards their car.

As they were driving off Jason said, "Holy Shit! I think the Frey boys had something to do with all this."

"Ya know, I do too. Let's go back over to the Frey farm and take a look around."

They arrived back at the Frey farm, parked the car and started a more serious search of the area. They were in different outbuildings when Jason yelled over for Pete. "Hey, come over here and take a look at this."

Pete arrived at the shed where Jason pointed at four brand new shovels from Ace hardware lined up together against a wall. Jason said, "Those are brand new, and it looks like they've only been used once or twice. Why would anyone need four shovels, unless they all were digging together somewhere?"

"Like a shallow grave?" Pete said softly.

"Like a shallow grave," Jason replied.

Pete went to his car and called the Lake George Sheriff's Office. After briefing the sheriff on the events at the lodge and farm, he told him that they had just reason to ask for a search warrant for the farm. The sheriff said he would get right on it and have the warrant by tomorrow morning.

He also asked the sheriff to track down the family of Sheriff Frey, since they all were probably born in the Lake George area. He also asked for information on David Short and if they would check with the local Ace hardware store and see if someone had bought four shovels within the last few weeks.

After more outside searching at the farm, with no interesting results, they drove back to Lake George and to the Holiday Inn. Pete called his office. "Jane, I want you to check all the airline flights into Albany for anyone named Frey within the last month. I'm looking for a couple guys named

Frey who may have flown in from Florida and another southern state." She said she would get right on it and get back to him as soon as possible.

Pete and Jason met for cocktails and another good dinner. After dinner Jason called Higgie and went through the same ole routine. "Oh, I miss you so much.. ... yadda, yadda, yadda."

The next morning Jason was up bright and early and excited about the information they had discovered. When he met Pete in the restaurant for breakfast, he was already on the phone. It took two cups of coffee before Pete finally hung up.

"Jason, my boy, things are looking up. Remember I told you Waller had flown to Zurich. Well, our agents talked to Samuel Rome about Andrews or the company having accounts in Zurich. He told them that Zurich was a favorite city of Andrews and that he had Swiss bank accounts in Zurich and flew there often. Perhaps Waller was on a little trip for Andrews. However, if he was, there is no record of Waller returning to the states."

By the time they got to the local sheriff's office, there was news about the Frey family. Sheriff Frey had two brothers, Donald and Tyce. Donald would be 53, Tyce 56. An internet search showed several Donald Frey's in St. Petersburg, Orlando, West Miami, Mount Dora, Sanibel Island, Lakeview and Sarasota.

Tyce Freys were also found in numerous other towns and cities: Oxford, Mississippi; Selma, Alabama; Little Rock, Ark; Memphis, Tennessee; and in Atlanta, Georgia. They were shocked to see the name "Tyce" in that many locations.

"Bingo! Pete said. "Isn't it interesting that two of the towns are the same two places where Dr. Waller had flown. My guess would be that our two brothers are from Sarasota and Little Rock. Ok, let's find out who these two guys are, if they are related to our local sheriff, and what they do for a living."

At that time one of the local deputies reported that, four weeks ago, a middle-aged man bought four shovels from the Ace Hardware Store and paid cash.

Pete said, "Well, that puts it into the right time-frame, but doesn't tell us who bought the shovels." He turned to the sheriff and said, "Have one of you men taken this hunting picture down to Ace Hardware and seen if any of the people there recognize anyone in this picture?"

While they were discussing the possibilities, the search warrant for the Frey farm arrived. Pete asked the sheriff, "Can we take some of your men to the farm and look for fresh dirt around the area. It probably wouldn't be too close to the farmhouse, but we will do the best we can."

The sheriff replied, "I'll get some men out there right away."

Pete's cell phone rang. It was Jane in his office.

"Pete, I have some news for you. I've got the names and dates of two men who few to Albany within the time frame you mentioned. Tyce Frey flew from Little Rock to Atlanta to New York City to Albany, and Donald Frey flew from Tampa to New York City to Albany."

"That's close enough for me. Our Donald, from Sarasota probably drove to Tampa for the flight. Good work, Jane. Now I want to know everything about Donald in Sarasota and Tyce in Little Rock."

"No problem boss.," Jane cheerfully replied.

Pete turned to Jason and the sheriff and said, "Ok, now we got three brothers, all together at the family farm, all hunting buddies of our missing Mr.Andrews. It looks like one of them probably bought four shovels from Ace Hardware. What we need to know is why they were digging. I suppose they could be burying money. However, it doesn't make any sense that anyone would bring money back from Swiss bank accounts and bury it at a farm in upstate New York. Maybe a better guess would be burying a body."

Pete's phone rang again. It was Jane. "Pete, I hope you're sitting down, I have some really terrible news."

"What?" exclaimed Pete.

"Samuel Rome's downtown apartment was just blown up, and his charred body found tied to a chair in the rubble. Our people say it looks like he might have been tortured before the explosion."

"Good Lord, when did it happen?"

"It happened about 9 o'clock this morning. His office says that yesterday he refused to see a couple of men who were very upset by his refusal."

"What did the men look like?"

"Middle Eastern was the description we were given. Pete, when you questioned Rome recently about Zurich, did you notice anyone else his in office or around the area that may have looked out of place?"

"I don't remember seeing anyone unusual. How would anyone know we were questioning him about Zurich? We were the only ones in the room."

"I don't remember anyone unusual, either, but my guess is that his office has probably been bugged ever since the OPEC countries lost one hundred million dollars. These days it's not very difficult to do. We should have thought of that and warned Rome."

"Jane, try to think if there is any way we can find out what Middle East guys are in New York. I know that there are many, but maybe your team can think of an angle to work with. Meanwhile, keep me posted on any police reports about the explosion. I assume they didn't find Mrs. Andrews in the rubble, did they?"

"They didn't find anyone else. There were a lot of people injured on adjoining floors, but no other deaths."

When he hung up, he reported the call to Jason and the sheriff.

Jason said, "That could have been me. That could have been Higgie.

We have got to get this solved before anything else bad happens."

"Calm down, we'll get it done," Pete said in a calming voice.

That was not enough for Jason. He called Higgie immediately.

"Hi there, how are you? Is everything ok? Seen any strange men hanging around your home or the office lately?" He was doing his very best to stay calm.

"What the hell are you talking about? What kind of strange men?"

"Don't get all excited! I was just asking."

"Jason, do you know something that I don't know, and should?"

"No, no, I just was a little concerned about where those men from the Middle East might be located…you know, the ones that came to my house that night."

"Jason, what is going on?"

"Samuel Rome was just killed this morning and the FBI thinks that whoever did it may have been from the Middle East."

"And you think that they may come after me?"

"Well, you are my girlfriend, and if they can't get to me, they might try contacting you."

"Jason, I'm hanging up now. I'm packing my suitcase and taking a vacation to my folks' home in California. I really don't need to be here."

"No, no. Settle down. They probably won't try to contact you, so don't worry about it."

"Don't worry about it! I received a telephone message on my answering machine here at work this morning. It was left last night. It was a man with a Middle Eastern accent who wants to talk to me. I'm getting the hell out of here!"

Jason interrupted, "I'll be on a plane this afternoon. This is not worth it. I love my company, but I love you more."

"Jason, I'm calling Clinton Byron. I'd feel much better with a FBI agent around me. You stay there. I'll keep in touch with you."

"Are you sure?" Jason blurted.

"Yes, I'm sure. You stay there and get this finished."

"Ok, you call Agent Byron. I'll call you later today."

There was not much for Pete and Jason to do in Lake George, so they went back to the Frey farm, where the police were searching for fresh dirt.

David Short drove up in his pick up and came up to Pete.

"Hi there, what's going on?"

"Well, Mr. Short, the police think someone may have been doing some digging on the property recently and they are trying to find out where."

"What they looking for?" Short said.

"We don't know what we're looking for, but we think it may have something to do with our missing man case."

"You think Mr. Andrews was here on the Frey farm?"

"Yes, we think he might have been."

"I didn't see anyone around here, but I was on vacation for a couple weeks."

"You were on vacation? When were you on vacation?"

"Well we just got home a couple weeks ago. My wife and I went on a two-week cruise down in the Caribbean. Mr. Frey gave it to us for all the hard work keeping the place up over the past several years. Had a great time…got sunburned, but didn't get seasick."

Pete excused himself from Short and called his office.

"Jane, I want you to send some agents to Jasper, and pick up Sheriff Ken Frey. I know he is very involved in Harold Andrews' disappearance. I just don't know quite how yet. Bring him to Albany and hold him."

"Ok, Pete, and I've got some information on your two Frey brothers. Tyce Frey is the vice president of an investment bank in Little Rock. He's married to a Jane Frey and they live in North Little Rock on Country Club Lane. He also owns a hunting cabin in Sturtgart, Ark."

Jane continued, "Donald Frey lives in Sarasota, Florida. He is a veterinarian employed by Ringling Brothers Circus. He is not married and lives on Midnight Pass, in Siesta Key."

"Jane, you're wonderful. That information fits into the puzzle perfectly. We have a man who knows everything about banking and moving money around the world and a man who knows everything about monkeys. I think we've got our men, but the only thing we don't have is the master prize, Harold Andrews. However, we may be standing on his grave at this very moment. Thanks, I'll get back to you."

When Pete hung up, Jason yelled. "I think they found something back in the woods. Let's go."

They jogged towards the woods where several men were gathered. One man said, "We were in this area and found a large pile of debris and leaves. When we moved away the debris, we found fresh dirt. It's an area of about 4 x 8 feet."

"Sounds like a grave to me," Jason whispered to Pete.

"Sure does. Ok, guys, let's see what we can find under this fresh dirt. Dig carefully, there may be a body."

After a few minutes one of the men said, "I think I've hit something and it's soft."

After a few more minutes, a body of a man was uncovered. The officers call for an ambulance and the coroner. The body was removed and taken to the morgue in Lake George.

CHAPTER 16

CLOSURE

It had been a long day and Pete was now back on the phone telling Agent Jane to contact the local authorities in Sarasota and Little Rock and have Donald Frey and Tyce Frey arrested. He wasn't quite sure what the charges were, but he knew they could be charged as soon as the local authorities identified the freshly exhumed body as that of Harold Andrews. He had asked that all of Harold Andrews' records be sent by fax to the county corner's office in Lake George to assure a valid identification.

Meanwhile Jason was on the phone to Indianapolis to reassure himself that the company image was still positive and intact. He was having nightmares about another client disappearing and Pinpoint, Inc. not being qualified enough to find him. Sometimes that insecurity carried over from real dreams to daydreams. So, he called home often to make sure all was well.

As they waited for the results from the coroner's office, Jason and Pete discussed the story of David Short. Was he really sent on a convenient cruise to get him out of the way, or was he in someway involved? Short seemed like an honest, hard-working guy, but surprises happen, and they weren't going to overlook anybody.

Everyone decided to take a break while the coroner's office did their work. Several hours went by. It was getting late. Perhaps everything would be on hold until tomorrow. Finally, Pete and Jason went back to the hotel, had a drink at the bar, then went back to their rooms and agreed to meet at 7:15 for dinner.

At seven p.m., Jason's phone rang in the room. He was almost ready to go to the restaurant and meet Pete.

It was Pete and he said, "Jason, I thought you would like to know. One of our agents took the hunting picture over to Jasper and showed it to Deputy Barns. He could not identify anyone in the picture as being the mysterious Gordon Dunbar. However, the agent also took Dr. Waller's picture from his Indiana driver's license." He continued, "Deputy Barns got really excited and yelled, 'That's him! That's Gordon Dunbar!'" "So, it looks like plain ole Dr. Waller was a little smarter that we thought he was. It's hard to believe that Waller could have played that role, but I guess he did. Ok, let's have dinner. I'll meet you in the restaurant."

During dinner, the conversation was vigorous. Was Dr. Waller in danger of being found by the OPEC guys? Do you suppose that they know he is in Europe? Did Samuel Rome tell them anything important before they blew him into little pieces? Would they get to Waller before the bad guys did?

They had dinner and went to bed.

At 10:45 Jason's phone rang. Higgie was in a panic.

"Jason, they're here! Do something! They're sitting in a car right across the street!"

"Calm down. Who's there?"

"I think it's the Middle Eastern men. I can hardly see them, but they've been there for thirty minutes!"

"Where's Clinton Byron?"

"He couldn't stay around the clock, so he left his car in front of my house."

"So they don't know that Clinton isn't there?"

"Hell, I don't know. How the hell would I know that?"

"Stay away from the windows. Call Clinton and call me right back!"

"Ok, ok." She replied.

Jason waited for six minutes. It seemed like an hour. His phone rang.

"What's going on?" He blurted out.

"Clinton is on his way and he's called for local help! Oh my God, Jason, they're not in the car!"

"Where are they?"

"I don't know. I didn't see them get out. I don't see them in front of the house."

"Are all your doors locked?"

"Yes. Jason, what do I do?"

"Do you have a gun?"

"Christ, no! What the hell would I be doing with a gun?"

"Well, shoot the bad guys for beginners! Stay calm, someone will be there in just a minute."

"Jason, I'm scared."

"Everything will be fine."

There was a long pause of silence on the phone and Jason said, "Higgie, you there? Talk to me Higgie!"

"Higgie, are you there?" There was no reply.

Suddenly there was a low whisper: "Jason, they are at my back door.

I can hear them trying to turn the doorknob. It's locked."

"Higgie, don't panic. Help is on the way."

She was almost sobbing now. "Jason, they're trying to get in the house!"

"Stay calm, Higgie. Go to the front of the house. If they come in the back door, go out the front door and run."

Silently she said:, "What if one is at the back and one is at the front?"

"Higgie, just do as I say, and do it now!"

She slid across the floor on her stomach and knees. In a moment she was in the front foyer. The front door was mostly glass, but she could not see if anyone was on the front porch. She slid to the door and put her left hand on the doorknob. The door was locked and she made sure she knew how to unlock it fast. She could still hear some sort of noise from the back door. She did not know if someone was in the house or not. She had turned the lights off in the house when she noticed the men in the car across the street. Now she could see very little in the house. She could maneuver around the house, but she could not see around the house.

She was there, frozen in time. She heard footsteps. At first she couldn't tell if they were outside or inside the house. She looked towards the doorway to the back of the house and then realized that the footsteps were coming up her front walkway.

She couldn't imagine that the Mid Eastern men would now be on the front walk. She braced herself, ready to let Clinton in the front door, or start running towards the back door.

There was a loud bang on the front door. She jumped back from the door and silently screamed.

Clinton shouted, "Higgie, are you in there?"

Tears ran down her face as she leaped to the front door. "Clinton!"

She yelled as she unlocked the door. Directly behind Clinton were a couple local police, with guns ready.

"Are you ok?" Clinton Asked.

"I am now," she replied, finally letting some air out of her lungs. "Sorry it took so long. I got here as fast as I could. Where are the guys you told me about?"

"Their car is right over there, across the street." As she pointed and spoke, her face looked shocked. "It was right there. God, it's gone! I swear it was right there!"

Clinton put his arm around her. "It's ok. It's ok."

She pulled herself together, brushed her hair back and said, "Thank you so much for coming. I don't know what I would have done without you.

I was talking to Jason.... Oh, my God...Jason...I left him on the phone in the back of the house." She turned on the lights and ran to the phone that was still lying on the floor.

"Jason, Jason, oh sweetheart, I'm sorry I left you on the floor!"

"Are you Ok?" he screamed into the phone.

"Yes, yes, I'm fine. Clinton is here and everything is fine."

"Well, damn it, you could have at least taken the phone with you when you went to the front door. I am a little interested in all this, you know!"

"I'm sorry, I'm sorry. I love you, I love you. I'm fine."

There was a long pause and Jason said, "What did you say your name was?"

After talking to Clinton and getting assurance that someone would be stationed outside her home all night, Jason made arrangements to talk to her again in the morning.

At 7 o'clock Jason received his wake up. He then immediately called

Higgie. She was still in bed, but sounded much better this morning.

She told Jason that the patrol car was going to follow her to work and stay in front of the company today. Feeling somewhat satisfied, they exchanged loving comments and Jason prepared to meet Pete.

At 7:30 a.m. Jason and Pete were both in the restaurant having coffee, planning the day.

Pete said, "We can probably go back to New York City today, I'm not sure what else we can do up here."

Jason replied, "Yea, I'd like to get back to Indy and get my life back together. I need to put everything back in order now that we've found Andrews."

Pete said, "Well, at least today we might be able to confirm what happened to Harold Andrews." Then his voice fell off to a muted "Maybe."

"What the hell do you mean, maybe?" Jason said firmly.

"Well I'm a little surprised that the body, in the grave, had all its parts together. When they went to the company to transfer the money, they could have just brought his head, or an eyeball and a hand to get through the security requirements. Taking Andrews down to his company alive, which is the other choice, would have been very risky. Someone could have recognized him. Of course, he might have been part of the scheme and knew how to get safely in and out of the company. Maybe after the transfer they came back to the farm and they decided they didn't need him anymore."

Jason replied, "Yea, but wouldn't they have to know something about getting the money out of the Swiss bank accounts after they transferred it?

Pete replied, "Sure, but they had a financial guy and could have gotten all that information, by force, before they put him in the grave."

"Oh, Jesus, Pete, I was all ready to put this all to bed, until you brought up all that. I was sure that we got everything straight and now you come up with all that crap."

"Well Jason, we'll just have to get one of the Frey brothers to talk. Then we'll have all the answers."

It was 8:10 when Pete's cell phone rang. It was the sheriff's office. "Mr. Donnelly, the sheriff would like to see you right away. How soon can you get to his office?"

"We can be there in 20 minutes."

"Yes sir, I'll tell the sheriff. Thank you."

Pete turned to Jason. "Well, that didn't sound good. Let's get down to the sheriff's office and see what the hell is up."

They reached the sheriffs' office at 8:40am and hurried in.

"You guy's want some coffee?" The sheriff said.

"Hell no, your call didn't sound too encouraging. What's going on? exclaimed Pete.

"Well, you both better sit down. It's going to be a long day."

"What! what!" Pete replied.

"The body we dug up yesterday isn't Harold Andrews. We're not sure who it is, but it's not Harold Andrews."

"Oh, Shit!" Pete murmured.

"Is it one of the Frey brothers?" Jason blurted.

"We have no idea," the sheriff replied. As far as we know it's just an unidentified body. Pete, did your agents in Florida and Arkansas arrest the brothers? If so, we could eliminate them as the victim?"

"I haven't talked to my office today, but I'll damn sure call right now." He walked out into the hallway to call Jane in his office.

"Jane, what about the Frey brothers, do we have them?"

"We've got both of them in custody…got them both last night.

"Damn!......I mean, great, I guess," he murmured

"What's wrong, Pete? You sound a little confused."

"Well, the body we found yesterday isn't Harold Andrews. I was kinda hoping it was one of the Frey brothers. That would at least tell us whose body was in the grave."

"Sorry, we've got them both. I guess I'm also sorry to say that they are both alive."

"Ok, back to the drawing board. Talk to you later. Thanks."

Pete went back into the sheriff's office and broke the news that whoever was in the shallow grave, it was not one of the Frey brothers.

Jason looked at Pete. "Well, of all the players, the only two that we know are missing are Trammell Waller and Harold Andrews. If it's not Waller, it's someone who stumbled upon the plot and was rewarded with a shallow grave."

"Trammell Waller," Pete whispered under his breath. "You don't suppose the body could be Waller?"

"Can't be Waller," Jason said. "As far as we know he's in Zurich or Europe somewhere. His passport would have told us if he had come back to the States."

Pete retorted, "Unless he came back to the States on a fake passport. You know, you can buy a lot of fake passports with one hundred million dollars and maybe he didn't want anyone to know that he was traveling back to the states."

Jason added, "And if he came back with the loot, maybe he didn't want to share it with the Frey brothers. Then the boys got a little upset and put him in the grave."

Pete snapped back, "Yea, then Andrews is still alive and could be somewhere in the states. They didn't need Waller, because they had Andrews. Or Andrews had them doing whatever he said."

The sheriff finally chimed in. "What if Trammell Waller never was in Zurich or Europe? What if he's been in that shallow grave ever since the money was stolen?"

Pete and Jason looked at the sheriff, both stunned.

"Oh, my God," Jason said. "We can't see the trees for the forest, or we can't see the forest for the trees, or whatever the hell it is."

"I think we better see if our body belongs to Trammell Waller, since it's not Andrews," Pete said with some urgency.

Pete called Jane again. "Jane, I need everything we've got on Trammell Waller; all his records. We need them quickly."

"Ok, I'll fax what we have to the sheriffs' office in Lake George."

"Great, that's where I am now." He hung up and stared at Jason.

Pete said, "I can't believe this never crossed my mind. I was so sure we had things all bundled up. So, if this is Trammell Waller, that only leaves the one and only Harold Andrews at large."

Jason replied, "So, maybe Wallers' passport and identification went to Sarasota, Little Rock and Zurich…but maybe not Waller. Maybe it was Andrews all along."

"How old and big is Waller?" the sheriff asked.

"If I remember correctly, Waller is about 51 years old, 6 feet tall, 200 pounds, gray hair and a small, pudgy tummy," Jason replied.

"And Harold Andrews?" The Sheriff asked.

Pete answered slowly, "47 years old, around 6 feet tall, 198 pounds, gray hair and a small, pudgy tummy."

Everyone stared at each other. Nobody said a word or moved a muscle.

Finally Pete spoke. "Ok, how about this? Harold Andrews had Waller killed after he removed the chip because there was no use to keep him around. Waller wasn't too sharp, so why give him a split of the pot. Andrews had the Frey brothers do all the dirty work and by the time we got involved, the brothers were spread all over the country. We've got to find out who was in that grave."

It was now around lunch time. Pete, Jason and the sheriff walked across the street to Mimi's Deli. Lunchtime went fast and soon they were all back in the sheriff's office. The fax machine produced the info on Trammell Waller and the sheriff had the papers rushed to the coroner's office.

Time seemed to move slowly as the three men talked about crime in the streets, Syracuse football, the Yankees and anything else to make the minutes go by quickly. Finally, at 2 p.m. the coroner's office called and confirmed that the body from the shallow grave was Dr. Trammell Waller.

Jason was the first to speak. "So, where in the hell is Harold Andrews and why did he give up a great financial life to steal money from himself?"

Pete stood up and said, "I can't take it anymore. I need some answers. Let's go talk to Sheriff Frey and see if he'll give it up. Maybe he'll give us some answers to all the questions we can't seem to figure out for ourselves."

The FBI agents had moved Sheriff Frey to Albany. Pete and Jason checked out of the Holiday Inn and headed towards Albany. During the one hour drive they conjectured every possible twist. They re-asked all the questions for the umpteenth time.

When they got to Albany, Jane called Pete to say that Donald Frey had given up his two brothers. Donald had simply said he wanted to lighten his sentence. He also mentioned that he really wasn't too fond of his beloved brothers and that Ken had pretty much screwed up the whole thing. He said that the day they transferred the funds, Ken was on Andrews' back about getting the money and didn't like the idea of waiting for Andrews to get the cash. He was sure that Andrews would just disappear and they would never hear from him.

By the time they reached the jail in Albany, they knew they had figured out most of the story. They were taken to Ken Frey's cell.

"Good afternoon, Sheriff. I hope you're comfortable," Pete quipped.

Ken Frey never looked up.

Jason added, "Would you like to tell us about what happened?"

"Nope," said Frey.

Pete leaned down next to the sheriff's ear and said, "Ever watch that TV show, Law and Order? When they'd catch the bad guy, then always gave him a chance to cooperate and ask the court to consider his cooperation. That might be something for you to think about. Donald already gave you and Tyce up to get a deal. You might as well get your own deal."

"Donald would do that," Ken snapped.

Pete smiled. "Well, I guess you haven't watched Law and Order.

That is always what the bad guy says, just before they put the noose around his neck. And the next thing he says is Oh God, I can't believe it."

"What did Donald say?" asked Ken.

"He said the three of you helped Andrews pull off the whole deal. He didn't say who actually killed Dr. Waller, but I'm sure he'll blame you or Tyce. It's just the way the story always goes."

"That asshole...all he knows is his precious animals. I knew he would buckle under if he was pressured. He's got no God damn spine! I didn't kill Waller. I just helped bury him after he was dead. I wasn't even in the room when he died. Nobody was going to miss him anyway. His wife was already dead and he had nobody. He did what he was supposed to do and after that Andrews said we didn't need him. I think Andrews actually did it."

"And Harold Andrews…where is he?"

"Hell if I know. He's in some God damn place in Europe, Switzerland or someplace. He got the hell out and left us here to take the heat!"

"How did he get out, without a passport?"

"Oh, he had a passport…Waller's. He had Waller's passport, drivers license, medical insurance card and even had his damn social security card."

"How did he get into the company to make all the transfers?"

Frey grinned. "Isn't it wonderful what $100,000 will buy? The guard on duty had been there for many years and had a lot of financial problems. He didn't blink an eye when Andrews told him that he would give him $100,000 to go into the men's room and stay there for a couple of hours, and keep his mouth shut. Can you believe that return, a $100,000 to get a hundred million? What a deal!"

"And what did you get?" Pete asked.

"Oh, all three of us got a million, except we haven't seen it. Andrews said he had to go to Europe to get the cash and would send it to us. I guess we are as dumb as we look. We all set up several bank accounts for ourselves and he was supposed to deposit the money in our accounts. We had to have several so there wouldn't be too much going into one account. It all was to be done by the end of this week."

Pete and Jason both stared at Frey and Jason asked, "And now the really big question...with all his success and money, why did he have to pull this little heist?"

"Aw, hell, he wasn't happy. He had a lot of money, but his wife was spending it faster that he could make it. He knew she was having an affair with some guy and making a fool out of him in the country club social circles. Most importantly, she told him that she was going to divorce his ass and take everything he had. The laws in New York don't always go the way of the husband, ya know. He figured he could just end it now by taking a hundred million out of his own funds...ninety-five million after expenses. Then he could disappear in Europe somewhere and start all over again. When he told us, it sounded like a good plan."

"And the chip?" Jason asked.

"That was the easy part. Waller planted the chip in Andrews some time ago. So he knew where it was in his body. There wasn't any problem getting it out. Tyce thought up the idea of putting it in a monkey and having the law chase it around South Africa. He said the body temperature of a monkey was about the same and nobody would figure it out. Waller could go to South Africa, buy a monkey, put the chip in and release it in a game park. Nobody had any idea that the park rangers would round up monkeys to sell for research experiments around the world. I'll be damned if our monkey didn't end up back in the states within days of releasing it. That was just a bad break."

Pete and Jason just sat there and looked at each other. All the sudden it all sounded so simple. Jason got up and left the room.

Pete asked Ken if there was anything else he wanted to tell him.

"Nope, I think you got the whole story. I knew Deputy

Barns couldn't handle the details of the car investigation. Hell, he didn't even ask Waller, a.k.a., Gordon Dunbar, what his address or phone number was."

Ken hung his head. "I had it all planned. A condo on the beach somewhere around Siesta Key Florida...wow, that sounded good. I can't say much for my worthless brother, Donald, but he sure lived in a beautiful area. All that sun and sand and no money worries...we all thought it was sure worth the shot."

Pete rose and turned to the cell door, walked out of the cell and never said another word to Ken.

Pete and Jason thanked the sheriff and drove back to the Holiday Inn.

In all the excitement this morning, they forgot to check out of the hotel.

"Do you want to spend the night or drive back to the city?" Pete asked.

"Let's go back. The sooner we get back, the quicker I can get to an airport and back to Indianapolis."

They checked out and drove back to the city. Pete took Jason back to the Crowne Plaza. It was late. Pete said, "Well, buddy, it's been one hell of a ride. I'll be down to Indy in a week or so to wrap things up. I think we're going to have to let someone else try to find Andrews in Europe. I'm sure our agency will be in contact with the Swiss officials and Interpol."

Jason shook his head. "You know, in all this time, I've really never asked you where you are from, or how you got into the FBI. I guess I was too busy thinking about the case and saving my company."

Jake smiled back. "Well, I guess I never offered the information. I'm originally from Memphis. I grew up in a neighboring town called Germantown,graduated from Germantown High School and went to Ole Miss in Oxford.

PINPOINT INC.

After Ole Miss I worked for the state for several years and applied to the FBI. Got the job and here I am in the big apple."

"Ever been married?" asked Jason.

"Yea, during my last year at Ole Miss. She was a great gal. We were married for three years before she was hit, head on, by a drunken driver just north of Oxford. She died at the scene. I never even dated much after that. But since you can't seem to find anyone, I guess I'm not the only looser here."

The both laughed, gave each other a jab to the shoulder, then a brief man's hug.

"Pete, I can't thank you enough for hanging in with me. I think since Andrews pulled this off himself, Pinpoint, Inc. won't suffer. And, since you actually look like Harrison Ford, I feel like I have been in a movie."

"Jason, you're a great guy and I've really enjoyed our friendship, even though we were always on business. I hope we can stay friends and keep in touch. Harrison Ford? Do you want my autograph?"

Jason laughed, they shook hands, gave another little man's hug and Pete drove off.

The next morning Jason was on an early flight to Indy. Higgie met him at the airport. The first thing out of his mouth was, "You know; I've been doing a lot of thinking. I just don't think I can live without being with you every day and every night. So, what do you say about that?"

"Is that a proposal?" She said with her sexiest voice.

"It is, if it will get you in bed, naked!"

"I'll let you know," she said with a big grin, and jumped into his arms.

"I'm at loss here. Is that a yes or a no?"

"Well, I'm not taking my clothes off in the middle of the airport and I don't see any beds, but, I think it's a yes."

The kiss was long and meaningful. Jason and Paula Higginbothem were officially engaged. She was also excited about having a regular last name, like Higgins. She could now just say Higgins and leave the damn "bothem" off.

On the way from the airport Jason told Higgie the entire story that unraveled in upstate New York. He admitted that Andrews had everyone fooled. Andrews had pulled off almost the perfect crime. He was tucked away somewhere in Europe with millions and would probably never be found for a long time.

'Higgie, my dear, we just might have to live with the fact that we lost our very first client."

"Well, my dear," she replied. "I think you're being a little hard on yourself. I think it's safe to say that Andrews lost himself and you put up one hell of a fight to find him."

"I knew I liked you for some reason. You're pretty damn smart," Jason replied. "So how long is an engagement supposed to last? Do I have to act like a fiancé or can I just go on and assume the role of a husband, with all its privileges?"

"You might want to just act like a fiancé. The word around the locker room is that they do a lot better," she replied with a raised eyebrow.

Two days later Jason had an urgent note on his desk from Pete.

It read: "Couldn't get you in your office or on your cell phone, you must have turned it off. Call me, it's urgent."

Jason called. When Pete's office answered, he was on another call. Jason asked to wait.

During the wait, Jason yelled for Higgie to come in his office and told her that something important must have happened. Maybe Tyce Frey had told them something new that helped the case.

Pete came on the line. "Jason, the world works in strange ways. Interpol has just contacted us. I hope you're sitting down."

"Geeze Pete, what is it?

"The Zurich police got a lead on a man using Trammell Waller's passport. Evidently the downtown Zurich Inter-Continental Hotel had to record the passport information upon check-in. When the hotel reported that a man had been murdered, execution style, the police found the passport and other documents in the room. The murder took place in the room, but the body was not discovered in the room.

The hotel is a massive, eight-story building with a drive-through porteco-chere. Across the front of the hotel are several flags, from various countries, hanging on poles that protrude from the building. The murdered man's room was just above the level of the protruding flag poles. The room was registered to a Dr. Trammell Waller, as the passport had stated.

Just outside and below the open window of Waller's room was the American flag. A ledge separated the windows and the flag poles.

Hanging upside down, from the base of the American flag, from a rope, was the headless body of a man. The body was hanging by the ankles. The rope was long enough to allow the body to hang just above the overhanging drive-through.

Perched on a concrete ledge, just left of the American flagpole was the severed head of Harold Andrews, a.k.a., Trammell Waller. Eyes open, looking straight ahead into the dark night.

Protruding from the blood stained corner of the mouth was a small piece of paper. When the police removed the paper they found words, hand written in Arabic. It took only minutes for the note to be translated. The note, in Arabic, read:

A gift to Allah.

End.